A youngster of sixteen or so jumped in front of Breckenridge, legs spraddled and his hand poised tautly over his gun. "Where do you think you're going?" the boy demanded.

"Over to help my friend," Breckenridge said. "Stand aside."

"Not for the likes of you, I ain't moving! You ain't no son of George Breckenridge. You're a liar!"

"Them are strong words. Now, step aside."

A sneer twisted his adversary's face. "Why don't you make me? Let's see how fast this son of George Breckenridge really is!"

The wild-eyed youth jerked his iron from its holster. Instinctively, Breckenridge acted. Whipping out his own weapon and diving to one side, he squeezed the trigger. . . .

KID BRECKENRIDGE

BERNARD PALMER

LIVING BOOKS
Tyndale House Publishers, Inc.
Wheaton, Illinois

First printing, December 1984

Library of Congress Catalog Card Number 84-51533
ISBN 0-8423-2059-8
Copyright 1984 by Bernard Palmer
Printed in the United States of America

1

The bleak prairie stretched across their field of vision, an endless profusion of parched buffalo grass and treeless open country, unmarred by the structures of man. To the right the level upland was cleft as though by some gigantic axe, causing a deep fissure that widened as it stretched away. The land greened noticeably as it dipped to the water source that was the lifeblood of the Rocking Seven spread. On the far side it struggled out of the ravine and upward in a series of granite outcroppings and broken hills toward the towering purple ridge that brooded on the western horizon.

It was midafternoon in July 1866, and a blight was upon the land; a blight as searing as the ache in the hearts of the sad quartet riding the dusty trail. An hour before, they had left the cemetery just outside of Weaverville, Wyoming Territory, and were moving slowly toward the Rocking Seven buildings. The ground was baked hard by the relentless sun and the well-shod hooves scarcely left a mark as the graying rider and his three youthful companions made their way across the brittle russet grass and sage that covered that section of the plains.

Sixteen-year-old John Breckenridge was sitting straight and stiff in the saddle, ignoring the sun and wind that bleached his hair and leathered his youthful skin. He was short and angular for his age, envious of Fletcher Ross who was nineteen. Fletch's torso was lean and wiry; as fast growing as a cottonwood sapling on the bank of a creek, its feet in the water and its leaves reaching upward for the cloudless sky. Fletch was just like John wanted to be, but wasn't.

Beside John rode his sister, Miriam: a slender, thin-faced seven-year-old who stared directly ahead. Her mild gray eyes were fixed on the distant horizon, and her expression, even when they talked to her, did not change. She seemed aware that some cataclysmic event was going on around her, but could not quite comprehend it.

Uneasily, John drew his attention away from his sister and glanced back at his stepfather. "Waddy?" he said.

Jerked from his thoughts, the older man pulled himself erect. "Yeah?" There was concern in his voice.

"Do you reckon Ma was hurting a lot?" the boy asked. "Toward the end, I mean." John heard his sister choke and saw a tight young fist lift to scrub at her eyes again.

Waddy Ross hesitated. His wife had been wasting away for six months with a disease called cancer that the doctor didn't seem to know much about. She had dropped in weight from a robust 146 pounds to less than 100 before her time to go. Although she didn't complain (she hadn't been the complaining kind), he suspected she had suffered more than anyone knew: especially John and Miriam. But it wouldn't do any good to tell her kids that. They were tormented badly enough as it was. Usually he was completely honest and forthright, but this time he decided it was best to stretch the truth a bit. Besides, he didn't know for sure she had been in pain.

"I don't reckon so," he mumbled.

Waddy's own son, Fletcher, broke in quickly. "You know better than that, Pa," he blustered. "She was hurting bad. Real bad."

John flinched. He dared not look at Miriam. He *knew* that would be enough to start the flow of her tears again. The lines about his mouth drew tight and his fist clenched on the reins till his knuckles whitened. That Fletch! Why couldn't he keep his big mouth shut? Things were hard enough for his sister without worrying about how much Ma suffered.

John wasn't the only one who was disturbed by Fletcher's outburst. Waddy Ross frowned his disapproval at his son. "Mind your tongue, boy!"

"It's the truth! She hurt bad. You could see it any time you looked at her."

"I said, shut up!" he rasped.

"All right." Fletcher mumbled. "I'll shut up. But I'm telling ya the truth. She was hurting bad."

John glared at Fletch, wishing himself a head taller and thirty pounds heavier. *One of these days,* he thought to himself, *that stupid Fletch is going to go too far! Then I'll make him sorry he ever opened that big mouth!*

John and young Ross had never gotten on too well; they hadn't from the first day he and his ma and Miriam moved into the Ross home. Actually, the trouble between them had started before Agatha Ross had died, when Waddy Ross and George Breckenridge first joined forces to start the

Rocking Seven. Then, when Agatha was gone, his own pa died and his ma and Waddy Ross decided to get married. Things between the two boys were suddenly a great deal worse. John was jealous of Waddy and Fletch resented having his new ma tell him what to do. Each took the recent events out on the other, as though he were the one responsible.

For a time John rode in silence beside his sister, trying to ignore her sniffling and an occasional muffled sob. He stared across the desolate grasslands, another matter disturbing him. He didn't know whether he should mention it or not, but it vexed him so much he had to speak about it.

"I've been pondering something," he said aloud. "What did that parson mean when he was talking about all them mansions in his Father's house?"

Waddy pulled a plug of tobacco from his pocket and cut off a chew. "Did he say that?"

"Sure as shooting."

A sigh came from the depth of the older man's being. "Hanged if I know." His stained teeth worked the tobacco methodically. "But your ma was a good woman. A mighty good woman. If anybody was to make it through them pearly gates it'd have to be the likes of her . . . . "

That eased the boy's pain slightly. The muscles in his face relaxed and he seemed to sag in the saddle, as though the agony of the last few days was suddenly giving way to a great weariness.

Waddy gathered in the reins without being conscious of his movements. He, too, was grieving for the loss of his wife, but at the moment his concern was for John and Miriam. It was hard for them, young as they were.

"I thought the parson done real good talking at her funeral," Waddy continued. "It would've made her plumb proud to know the kind things he said. And they was true. Every one of them!"

As his pa spoke, Fletcher's face darkened. "What's it with you, anyway?" he demanded. "Have you plumb forgot *my* ma?"

"Course not!" Waddy blurted. He had been blessed beyond measure by having *two* good women. But how could he explain that to his own hot-headed son? He had loved both Agatha and Emily more than he loved himself. He would gladly have taken the place of either, if they could have lived.

"You wouldn't understand," he muttered lamely.

"I understand, all right!" Fletcher exploded. "I know now where Ma and me stand with you. Way down at the bottom of the pile." As the words snarled from his lips he dug his spurs into the buckskin's flanks. The big horse leaped forward into a dead run, his powerful legs pounding the prairie.

Waddy stared helplessly after Fletch. There had been no cause for his taking off like that. Waddy didn't know what was getting into the boy; he was harder to handle every day. There was a wild, uncontrollable streak in him that would not be brought under subjection.

But it was Emily's boy who needed his attention right then. John had become a second son to him in the six years since George had been killed. As he looked over at the boy, he noticed tears gleaming hotly in John's eyes, trickling down his cheeks.

"Are you all right?" Waddy asked.

John swallowed hard. "Waddy, was . . . was Fletch right about Ma suffering so bad?"

"What would *he* know about it?" They rode on in silence.

John swayed miserably in the saddle. For some reason his heart ached for Waddy Ross. Ma had explained to him how it came that she and Pa's partner on the ranch were going to be married. Miriam was too young to understand. But they were alone after Pa died, and Waddy and Fletch were alone. They needed someone to keep house and she needed someone to do a man's work. And, living on the same ranch as they were, it seemed that getting married was the only practical solution.

But John figured there was more to it than that. Ma had been happier after she and Waddy got married than he had seen her since Pa died. It bothered him at first, noticing her cheeks flush and her eyes brighten when Fletch's pa came into the room. He thought she wasn't being true to his pa and that she wouldn't love him and Miriam any more, but that didn't last long. He saw how wrong he was and realized that Waddy loved them as much as he did his own son. John soon found himself thinking almost as much of the gruff, red-haired giant of a man as Ma did.

Waddy Ross had a quick smile and a heart as big as his massive frame. Everybody liked him, and the better John got to know his stepfather the more he understood why his ma loved Waddy. As early as John could remember the Ross family had lived on the Rocking Seven with his own family. But it was not until Ma had married the big rancher that the boy really came to appreciate his stepfather.

There didn't seem to be anything Waddy couldn't do, even though his fingers were twisted and slowed by rheumatism. He could throw a loop faster or take down a bigger steer or ride a meaner bronc than anyone else in Wyoming Territory, John decided. And, from what he had learned by listening to talk nobody knew he heard, Waddy was good at gunslinging, too.

Waddy Ross and George Breckenridge hadn't said much about their days on the trail, but John had overheard them talking when he was supposed to have been asleep. He was fascinated by the tales, and frightened, too. It was scary just to hear them, and he would often lie in bed at night thinking about them. He decided what he was going to do when he grew up: He would hit the trail as soon as he was old enough to be on his own. Once he got money enough, he was going to buy a six-gun of his own, a Colt Peacemaker just like Pa used to pack. And he would practice and practice and practice until he was as fast as his pa had been.

Only there was never enough money for him to buy a gun. The family had trouble enough scrounging for what they needed. John had a rifle he was learning to shoot, but as the days and weeks and months passed, his daydream of roaming the plains with a six-gun in each hand began to dim. Before long he almost never thought about getting a handgun of his own.

But now that his ma had died, he thought once more of leaving the ranch. *If it weren't for Waddy and Miriam I would get my stuff together and set out for Denver or Cheyenne or the Texas cattle trails,* he muttered inwardly. He would rid himself of Fletch and the new agony that gripped

11

him. He had the feeling that the ache in his heart would stay behind if he ran. But he realized he could not leave. At least not right now. For him to go would only make things worse for Waddy and Miriam and he couldn't do that.

Half an hour later the weary riders approached the ranch buildings. The house was a sprawling, one-story structure built with lumber hauled in from Cheyenne. The clapboard siding had never known the protective touch of paint and was badly weathered. The chimney lacked a good foundation and was standing slightly askew.

Although Emily Ross had been too ill to take care of things for only the past six months, the buildings already showed the absence of a woman's hand. A glass in one of the bedroom windows had been broken out and replaced by wood, and the back step had started to crumble and was propped up with a rock. The pole barn sagged at one corner until the door would not close completely, and there was a huge pile of manure at the back. Ordinarily Waddy would have had Fletcher and John haul it away regularly and spread it on the garden and wheat field, but ever since his wife took sick he hadn't had the heart for taking care of anything.

The disconsolate trio reined in near the kitchen door and Waddy and Miriam dismounted. "Take the horses out to the barn and feed and water them, John. Miriam and I'll go in and see if we can fix something to eat." Waddy managed a thin smile.

John didn't think he would ever be able to eat again, but he didn't say that to Waddy. He dismounted and led the horses to the barn where he unsaddled them and rubbed them down. Then, when they had cooled from the long, hot ride, he took them to the tank for water. Fletch made fun of the way he cared for a horse. He said John was a regular old woman when it came to fussing with some two-bit nag and that John's mount got better care than most people. But that didn't bother John. His pa had taught him to take good care of his horses. "The time may come," George Breckenridge had said, "when that extra burst of speed, good conditioning, and care might make the difference between keeping your scalp where it belongs or getting a bullet in your back."

John fed the horses and should have gone inside, but he lingered in the barn, postponing the time when he would have to return to the house. Now that he was home, that terrible, sick feeling churned wildly in the pit of his stomach. He didn't know whether or not he could bring himself to go into the little cabin Ma used to keep so clean.

Every room reminded him of her. She had made the curtains for the living room and hooked the rug for the floor. She had sewn the quilt for his bed and had darned his socks and patched his overalls. So often, when he came in from doing chores, had she been standing at the stove cooking, that he almost expected to see her there now. Even when she was sick and confined to her bed he hated to go into the kitchen because of all the pleasant memories it held. Now that she was gone it would be even worse.

John was still wrapped in his misery when the door creaked and a wedge of light pushed a portion of the darkness away, revealing the hindquarters of Waddy's big gray and the hay-strewn ground that served as a floor. A tall, slight figure filled the doorway, silhouetted against the faint streaks of gray in the sky behind him.

"What're you doing?" Fletcher Ross demanded.

"Nothing." John didn't feel much like answering.

Fletch led his own sweating saddle horse into the weary building and tied him at a manger. "Got the chores finished yet?" he demanded belligerently.

John didn't know how Fletch was able to make him so mad just asking a simple question, but he did. It was difficult for John to control his temper. He turned away and that should have been the end of it, but Fletcher wouldn't stop. "If they ain't done, get with it! We ain't got all day!"

John's head came up defiantly. "Waddy said I didn't have to help with the chores tonight."

"That's a lie!"

"Go ask him!"

Fletch snorted. "Your ma ain't coming back, no matter how you moan and groan about it. She's *dead!* So there ain't no use carrying on the way you've been doing!"

John fought against the sudden surge of tears and turned to curry the big gray. Fletcher grabbed him by the arm and spun him around, snarling, "Don't you turn your back, Breckenridge. I'm talking to you!"

John jerked away, his lithe torso trembling. "Keep your hands off me!" He expected Fletch to swing at him and was so angry he didn't care. However, his stepbrother ignored his defiance.

"Has Pa talked to you yet?"

John's eyes narrowed. "About what?"

"When you're going to be moving on."

"Moving on?" John had thought about leaving, but in truth, it scared him. He had figured on staying at the Rocking Seven at least till he was grown.

"Yeah. When're you getting outta here? You oughta know that Pa never thought nothin' of your ma, or you, or Miriam, either. He only married her because he felt sorry for you."

"I . . . I don't believe it!"

"Ask him! If he tells ya the truth, he'll say he doesn't want you no more. And why should he? You'd just be eating our food and riding our horses and getting in our way!"

John's cheeks blanched and his lips trembled. It shook him, he had to admit, but this time Fletch had gone too far. "That ain't true and you know it!" he challenged.

"Are you calling me a liar?"

John exploded with a ferocity that caught his taller, older adversary off guard. Jamming both hands against Fletch's chest he shoved him away so savagely Fletch tripped and sprawled backwards on the hay. He hit his head against one of the poles that supported the barn walls and for a moment blinked stupidly. John stared down at him. He felt no exultation. Only amazement that he had been able to accomplish something he had dreamed of doing for so long.

Fletch shook his head to clear the cobwebs. As he did so a great anger surged within him and rage gleamed in his eyes.

In that moment John realized the bigger lad was about to get up. The fight was not over; it had just begun. So he waited, cheeks flushed and fists clenched for action. Bellowing with anger, Fletch scrambled to his feet, lunging at his youthful foe. His long arms swung wildly as he attempted to land a blow on John's jaw. He couldn't stand the humiliation of being put on the ground by a kid little more than half his size. So he charged in, bent only on destroying his hated antagonist. John leaped nimbly to one side. He was small but quick, and in superb condition. As he avoided Fletch's blow he threw a short, punishing right that caught his stepbrother on the side of the head.

Fletch swore viciously. "I'll *kill* you for that!" He swung a bruising left, catching John on the shoulder. The younger boy stumbled backward and almost fell before catching himself and scrambling upright. That moment gave Fletch the advantage he had been seeking. He came crowding in, fists ready. Then, about to throw a punch, his hand snaked out instead, grabbed John by the arm and jerked him forward. As he did so, he released him suddenly. The change of tactics was befuddling. John went flying over the hay, crashed into the wall, and stumbled backward against one of the horses. The startled animal, made nervous by the rough and tumble battle, lashed out with a hind foot, catching John on the hip.

Excruciating pain shot up the boy's spine from the point of impact, and he went down cracking his head on a loose board. Blackness enveloped him and all was silent. He did not see Fletcher standing over him or hear Waddy Ross come limping to the door.

"Fletch!" the older man cried. "What's going on?"

2

Waddy Ross quickly knelt beside John and laid a hand on his forehead. Concern darkened his bronzed features. "John," he murmured. "Do you hear me?"

The boy stirred slightly but his stepfather was uncertain whether or not he was conscious. John did not open his eyes and made no move that would indicate he was awake.

The grizzled rancher looked up, his fearsome stare gripping his son. "Fletch," he demanded in a voice little above a whisper. "What was this all about?"

Fletcher withered under the cold, penetrating eyes. "I don't know, Pa," he said defensively. "I swear I don't know what got into him."

"You two were fighting. I could hear it from the house!"

"It weren't *my* doing. I don't know what happened to him. We was talking, nice as you please, when he plowed into me like an old she-bear! I *had* to defend myself. Honest, Pa! I didn't want to hit him, especially after all him and Miriam's been through. But I had to. He'd have plumb killed me if I hadn't fought him off!"

"You're lying!"

Fletch snapped erect, eyes cold with anger.

"I might've knowed you'd take *his* part. Ever since you married that ma of his you've put me down like I was nothing. Won't even believe me when I tell you the truth!"

Waddy spat contemptuously at his son's feet. "Shut up and give me a hand. We'll settle this matter later."

They carried John into the house and laid him on the bed that had been his ma's until two days before. Miriam pushed up beside Waddy.

"What is it?" she asked, her words trembling. "What happened?"

"He'll be all right. He fell and hit his head." The instant he spoke Waddy realized he had lied to her. The truth stabbed into him. When he could speak again he sent her to the kitchen for water. "We've got to get John washed up."

"*I'll* get the water!" Fletch exclaimed, starting for the door.

"Miriam will help you."

They left the room together and Waddy continued to examine the lithe young body.

"Don't think he's got any busted bones," he muttered to no one in particular, "and he's going to be a mighty stiff and sore for a few days. I expect he'll probably have a bad headache for awhile."

By this time Fletch and Miriam were back in the room. Now that Waddy had seen the extent of his stepson's injuries, fury as cold as a long winter night wrapped its tentacles about him. His gaze came up to meet that of his son.

"It's too bad he didn't tear your head off, Fletch. I've never been so shamed as I am right now. You fighting your own brother who's three years younger and don't weigh as much as you by thirty pounds. I oughta take a club to you!"

"He ain't no brother of mine!"

Miriam, who had been standing silently beside Waddy, looked up, hurt reflecting in her solemn young eyes.

"Shut up," Waddy ordered savagely, motioning quickly down at Miriam. "Understand?"

Fletcher's cheeks flushed and he was mumbling under his breath as he stormed into the other room.

Hesitantly the girl directed her attention from her stepbrother to the great, shaggy man who was the only pa she had ever known. "Why doesn't Fletch like John and me?" she asked, her voice trembling.

"He likes you," he said. "He likes you both. Don't pay no attention to what he says. He's just upset about your ma."

Miriam knew that wasn't true, but she didn't say anything.

Waddy Ross hobbled into the kitchen and got some cloths and another bucket of cold water. With Miriam hovering silently nearby, he sat beside John's bed and put cold compresses on the boy's smooth forehead. He didn't know whether they would do any good, but he remembered from way back that his own ma had put a lot of faith in that kind of treatment.

Fletcher had gone outside and didn't come back for two hours, but Waddy scarcely noticed that his son was not there. He decided he would wait till morning before sending Fletch for the doctor.

The hands on the clock seemed to have forgotten to move, so slowly did they creep past the numbers while John lay motionless on the bed.

Darkness filled the room, save for the feeble rays of the kerosene lamp on the dresser that cast long, grotesque shadows across the quilt and over to the brass headboard. John's youthful features were ashen and only his labored breathing revealed that he was still alive. A knife twisted in Waddy's inner being every time he looked down at the injured boy.

Miriam moved restlessly about the room. She sat at the foot of her brother's bed for as long as she could, then got up and wandered to the dresser where she studied her own pale reflection in the mirror.

"You look awful tired," Waddy said. "Don't you think you ought to go to bed?"

Her gaze lifted slowly to find his. "Is . . . is John going to be all right?"

He swallowed hard and hoped he sounded convincing. "Sure he is."

"I . . . I couldn't stand it if something happened to him, too. He's all I got!"

"No he ain't." The big man looped an arm awkwardly about her shoulder. "You got me."

"I know." Her smile flashed weakly. "But I. . . ."

Waddy nodded. He knew what she meant and could understand. She put an arm around his waist and for a moment felt comfort from the embrace. Then, without speaking, she went solemnly into her bedroom.

"Pa," she called after a time. "Pa?"

"Yes?"

"Could you come in?"

He squeezed the excess water from the cloth in his hand, placed it on John's forehead, and went into the room where Miriam was lying in bed. He

20

stood for a moment beside the iron bedstead. The lamp was still lighted, casting long shadows on the opposite wall. She reached up with her hands and pulled him down to her. "Ma always tucked me in."

"I know." He fumbled uncertainly with the covers, pulling them up under her chin and kissing her on the cheek. "How's that?"

"She always prayed with me, too."

He hesitated. "I ain't much on this praying business."

"I can help you."

There was a long silence that seemed to fill the grieving ranch home.

"Pa?"

"Miriam?"

"Ma told me if I would give my heart to Jesus, I would go to heaven to be with her. Is . . . is that the way it is?"

Waddy swallowed at the lump in his throat. "Iffen your ma told you that," he blurted, "it's got to be the pure truth. She was one of the most truthful women I ever saw." Miriam smiled, tears glistening in her eyes.

Waddy didn't sleep that night. Methodically he changed the compresses and, when the water felt warm to his gnarled fingers, he hobbled out into the yard and pumped more. He didn't hear Fletch come in, but when he went for more water some time after midnight, his son was sitting at the kitchen table, staring off into space.

"How's John doing?" Fletch asked.

Waddy glared at him.

The sun was up when weariness finally overtook the exhausted rancher and he leaned forward to rest his head on the bed. He hadn't been in that position long when he felt the boy stir. The movement was so restricted he was not certain he had felt anything at all. But his keenly tuned senses jarred him wide awake at the slight twitch of the bruised and battered body.

In the bright morning sunlight streaming through the window, John looked even more weak and helpless. Pain stabbed Waddy's heart, but as he stared down at his stepson, John's eyelids trembled.

Waddy reached out and touched him clumsily. "How do you feel, son?"

John was awake enough by this time to recognize the kindly voice. "Hello, Pa."

"Feeling better?"

"I don't know." He raised a hand uncertainly to brush it across his eyes. He was trying to figure out where he was and what had happened. He was aware only of the pain where he had been kicked, and the throbbing, racking ache in his head that blurred his vision and caused waves of nausea to sweep over him. As he battled to sort things out, he began to realize where he was.

"What am I doing here?"

At first Waddy did not answer. He reached out and smoothed the quilt with his powerful, calloused fingers, the way John's ma used to do. "We'll talk about that later."

"But . . . but this is *Ma's* room!" Panic tightened his voice.

"Don't you remember?" the man by his bed asked, miserably.

John raised himself on one elbow and clutched Waddy's powerful arm with his free hand. "What's happened to Ma?" he demanded harshly. "Where is she?"

Hurt leaped to the big man's tired eyes. "We'll talk about that later." His voice was choked with emotion. "Now you'd better go back to sleep. You got yourself hurt a mite."

But John was not to be put off so easily. "What happened to Ma?"

Waddy got up abruptly and left the room, but John scarcely noticed that his stepfather was gone. He lay back on the bed weakly, trying to force his mind to function. There were things he had to remember. But it was no use. His head seemed to ache worse when he tried to think, and his mind refused to dredge up any memories.

After a time Waddy returned and remained beside John till he was certain that he was sleeping soundly again. A great load left the weary, grieving man. He didn't think he could have borne the loss of both Emily and John so close together. He was thankful that he wouldn't be called upon to withstand such a catastrophe. Yet, one burden still remained. It had to be taken care of before the day was out.

Waddy was one of those simple, direct men who had to wade in and settle things as they came up. He could not allow them to go unresolved in the vain hope they would disappear.

This time, however, he had a problem he wasn't sure he knew how to handle. It beat all, the things a man was forced to face up to. Take a cow that had to be dehorned or hay to be put up or wood to be split and he could do it as easily as saddling a well-broken horse. A man was used to that sort of thing. But a fight between two of the three people in the world who meant anything to him was more than he was prepared for.

He went over to the stove and started frying

23

ham and potatoes and eggs for breakfast, still pondering the problem. He couldn't allow things to go on the way they were. It wouldn't be fair to John for him not to take a hand in it, and unless he did the trouble would only get worse. But that wasn't all; he had Fletch to think about, too. His son had never been able to accept Waddy's marriage to his partner's widow, and had done everything he could to make things miserable for everybody. What could Waddy do to straighten out the matter without making things worse?

He was still at the frying pan, his mood as black as the old cookstove, when the outside door opened and his son stormed in. Anger and resentment twisted Fletcher's young features.

"Where've you been?" Waddy demanded irritably.

"Out doing the chores. Where'd you think?"

"Don't talk so loud. You'll wake John and Miriam."

"Sounds like they're the only ones you *care* about!"

His pa did not answer.

"Breakfast ready?" Fletch sneered.

"You've got eyes. What does it look like?"

The lean, angular nineteen-year-old pounded across the room, spurs jangling noisily against the rough pine floor. He whipped a kitchen chair from the wall, jerked it around, and swung his leg over the seat to straddle it, leaning forward into the straight wooden back. "I've gotta talk to you, Pa."

Waddy fixed a bleak, cold stare on his son. "I've gotta talk to you, too, but it's going to wait till we've eaten breakfast."

Fletcher paid no attention to him. "What's

going to happen around here, now that your wife's dead?"

"What do you mean by that?" Waddy's voice was deadly calm; it contained the tone that had struck terror into the hearts and minds of those he had faced in the days when his gun was for hire.

"John and Miriam ain't a-going to keep on living here, are they? Now that their ma's dead, I mean. We ain't going to have to put up with them from now on, are we?"

Deliberately Waddy scooped the last of the eggs on the plate and hobbled over to the table. He set the plate down and faced his son. "Fletch," he rasped, "that ain't none of your business."

"But I . . . ."

"I don't wanta hear another word outta you. We'll do our talking outside when we've finished eating."

"I want to talk now." Fletch got quickly to his feet and moved forward.

"Turn that chair around and sit at the table proper-like," Waddy ordered. "And keep that mouth of yours shut. We ain't going into this any more till after breakfast."

Reluctantly the boy did as he was told, grumbling that he was not hungry.

"You'd best eat," his pa warned him. "You might not feel much like it when we get through." They finished the meal in silence.

Fletch knew better than to challenge his pa—especially right then when his mood was as ugly and unpredictable as a summer thunderstorm. So the boy remained at the table, toying with his food and feeling sorry for himself. When his pa had finished the last of the ham and the dishes were washed and dried, Waddy plodded clumsily toward the door, motioning his son to follow.

"Where we going?" Fletch asked uneasily.

"Out where we won't bother John and Miriam if I get to talking loud!"

"I might've knowed you'd be a-thinking about them!" his son complained. "I'm your own flesh and blood, but you don't care nothing about how I feel or what happens to me. All that matters to you is Miriam and John! I'm sick of it!"

"Shut up and do as I say!"

Obediently, the boy followed his pa out the door and in the general direction of the barn. The day was still young but the sun was well up, and shadows stretched out from the buildings and fence posts that made up the corral. When they reached a spot some distance from the house Waddy grasped Fletcher's arm with a viselike grip.

"I don't want to have to tell you again, Fletch," he rasped. "You've got to quit pestering that boy!"

"And if I don't?"

"You can saddle your horse and move on. And right now I don't care much one way or t'other, which you do!"

Hurt clouded the young man's eyes. "You always have taken his side. I'm your son! Remember?"

"I ain't taking nobody's side. But I can't have you giving John and his sister trouble. What's the matter, Fletch? Ain't we had enough grief around here lately without you making things worse?"

Fletcher continued to complain bitterly, and John, just waking, heard his stepbrother's angered voice and remembered: There had been a fight between him and Fletch. He had been jerked or pushed into the heels of Waddy's blue-roan and had been kicked savagely. His head slammed into something hard behind him and he blacked out, regaining consciousness only a short time before.

He had been lying in bed trying to sort out the jumbled incidents of the past few days when Fletch came into the kitchen. John heard only snatches of the muffled conversation that followed and what he did hear, his befuddled mind twisted into something far different from what was actually said. In his confusion, John thought Waddy didn't want him any more. The way he understood it, the gray-haired rancher had promised to take care of him and Miriam only because their ma asked him to. Fletch was right after all. Waddy *would* be relieved if he wasn't around.

If that was the way things were, he'd leave. He would like to take Miriam with him; Waddy probably didn't want her, either. But he knew he couldn't manage to look after himself and her, too. If he was out of the way, they might be happier about having Miriam. It was different taking care of a girl. It wouldn't be long till she would be able to do a lot of the work around the house and earn her keep.

John didn't know for sure where he would go. He might head for the Texas cattle trails, looking for a job as a drover. Waddy had always said he was right good with cattle.

Thinking about such things made his head ache worse than before and he closed his eyes and tried to force such thoughts from his mind, at least till he was well enough to leave. Yet the thoughts continued to come back to torture him. He had been rejected—betrayed. But, as soon as he was on his feet and able to ride again, he would be gone. Then they wouldn't have to worry about having *him* around.

3

As the days passed, John's head cleared and the soreness began to leave his hip. By the middle of the following week he was able to walk with only a slight limp, a grim reminder of the trouble between himself and Fletcher Ross. Guilt rose within him as he considered Fletch and Waddy's resentment and realized he wasn't even able to help with the chores.

At first he was too weak to do anything, but as his strength returned he tried to do what he could. Fletch saw him go out to feed the calves and scowled, even more sullen and morose than before, but he didn't argue the way he had in the past. John had almost finished feeding the young calves when Waddy saw him.

"How many times do I have to tell you to leave the work to Fletch and me?" he growled.

"I want to do my share."

"You'll get a chance to do your share when that hip's healed. Now get back to the house before I take a strap to you."

John limped back to the log building where Miriam was finishing the dishes. He could do things like feeding the calves and taking care of the horses, but it warmed his heart to know that Waddy thought enough of him to be concerned about his working before his hip was well.

John laid his plans carefully. His ma had given him Pa's saddle and rifle and always said he would get the well-worn Colt Peacemaker when he was old enough to learn to use it. He would take those things and the money she kept in the extra sugar bowl in the cupboard. He didn't know where she got the money. It was always scarce around the Rocking Seven. But John figured it was hers and taking it wouldn't be stealing.

He would have to take Rusty, too. Waddy always talked as though the big, raw-boned sorrel belonged to John but Rusty carried the Rocking Seven brand. That meant John could be accused of horse stealing if they caught up with him. But he couldn't imagine Waddy doing that. Someday he would come back and pay his stepfather for what he was taking. With that he tried to close his mind to the nagging uneasiness of his conscience and thought only about getting away from the ranch.

He decided he would take off from home as though he were riding over to a neighboring spread. Then, when he was several miles away and in the hard prairie clay where Rusty would be more difficult to track, he would double back to Weaverville, buy supplies, and be on his way. With plenty of everything, he would be able to strike out across country, putting more distance between himself and the ranch before Waddy, Miriam, and Fletch learned he was gone.

He would travel hard and fast the first several days. When he was certain he had outdistanced Waddy, or anyone else who might be pursuing him, he would find a good place and stop to rest his horse. No need to punish Rusty by pushing on, without giving him a chance to feed and get his strength back. After a rest, he would have decided where to go and what to do. John hadn't yet settled those matters in his mind.

He didn't tell anyone what he was planning—not even Miriam. As the eve of his departure approached he tried hard to act normal, but was afraid his stepfather would sense something was wrong. His heart was hammering fiercely and he felt a wave of expectation and dread sweep over him.

"You're mighty quiet tonight, John," the grizzled rancher said, his eyes narrowing. "Something troubling you?"

John began to tremble inside. "Not that I know of," he mumbled.

"You can't keep on grieving. Your ma wouldn't want that. You've got your life to live."

He nodded. It was difficult, but he managed a weak smile.

"That's better." Waddy sat down, poured a saucer of coffee from his cup, and blew on it. "Things are in good shape around here and Fletch can look after what needs doing for the next three or four days. How about you and me riding off into the hills and seeing if we can get ourselves some meat?"

"Pa," Fletch protested. "You can't leave me alone with all the work!"

Waddy ignored his protest. "You and Miriam can go some other time. Right now I believe John needs to get away for some hunting."

The boy winced.

The older man read the dismay on his ashen-gray features. "What's the matter?" he asked, disappointed at the boy's reaction. "Don't you want to go?"

"It ain't that," he stammered. "It's just. . . ."
He allowed his voice to trail off, not wanting to
give himself away.

"It's like I said, you've been moping around
here long enough. And your hip's healed so that
ain't an excuse no more. . . . Your ma would want
you to do things and be happy." Waddy finished
his saucer of coffee and poured another. "I think
a little hunting trip'll be just what you need. . . .
And I know for a fact that we can use the meat.
We'll get our gear together after supper."

John watched miserably while Waddy got out
their bedrolls and set out the grub they would
need.

"It's about time you start learning to use
your pa's six-shooter, too. We'll take that along."
As he worked he continued to talk, not even noticing that John remained strangely quiet.

Seeing his stepfather so excited about the
hunting trip stabbed remorse into John's heart
and for an aching moment or two he wondered if
he would have the courage to go through with his
plans. But he *had* to. This was just a show—a
pretense on the part of Waddy. He was trying to
make John believe he really wanted him to stay.

The rancher got the gear together, then set
out the rifles and handguns. As he worked he
seemed happier than he had been since his wife
died. But John was still determined to leave; the
hunting trip changed nothing. It was just a diver-
sion, part of an act to show that he was welcome
at the Rocking Seven. He had made up his mind
to leave and nothing was going to stop him.

That night, an hour after he heard Waddy
and Fletcher's heavy breathing, the boy pushed
back the covers quietly, slipped out of bed, dressed,

and tiptoed to the ladder that led down from the loft where he and Fletcher slept. He got the Sharps rifle, strapped the heavy Colt to his waist and took the money from the sugar bowl. There was more than he had remembered and he wanted to count it, but he didn't dare. At any moment someone might wake up and hear him.

At the door he hesitated and almost turned back to Miriam's room for a last look at her, but changed his mind. If he was discovered now, everything would be ruined. So he slipped out of the house, sneaked across to the barn, and saddled Rusty for the long, hot ride.

The six-shooter weighed heavily at his hip and he was very conscious of it as he mounted and turned toward the Slash Anchor. His heart was hammering fiercely against his ribs and his breath came in quick, shallow stabs. Once or twice he looked over his shoulder at the slumbering ranch house. For one brief instant doubt seized him and he wondered if he should go back. There was something final about running away like this, as though he were closing the door on a great part of his life.

The night was blanketed in clouds as he rode away from the buildings. Lightning forked the western horizon, just above the great, distant hills. He shivered and felt the bedroll tied to the back of his saddle. His slicker was in there, along with his heavy coat. He doubted he would even have thought about taking them had Waddy not gotten them out for the hunting trip.

He had been bold in planning his departure, but now that he was on his way his courage melted. What would he do when he was out of money and had nothing to eat? What if outlaws crossed his path or a renegade band of Sioux or Blackfeet attacked? He could shoot straight. Waddy had seen to that. But facing a thief bent on stealing his horse or a vengeful Indian determined to take his scalp was something else. He wondered how he would measure up.

On a little rise he stopped and wheeled Rusty about to look down on the buildings. At first he could scarcely make them out in the darkness, but as he stared the wind moved the clouds and a shining crescent of moon showed through. He could see the stern lines of the house and the squat little barn with the corral behind it. Even the well midway between the buildings was visible. For several minutes he remained stationary, emotion churning within. Then he clucked to his horse and rode off, fighting against loneliness and fear.

For two or three miles he remained on the trail so Waddy and Fletch would have no difficulty in tracking him. Then he switched to firmer ground where the tracking would be more difficult. Topping the highest ridge between the two ranches, he turned at a right angle to make his way along the granite outcropping. From there he went down to the creek and rode into the water for half a mile or more to further obscure his trail. He knew that would not deceive Waddy for long, but it should slow him some.

A chill swept over John. He didn't know why he was being so careful. Waddy wasn't going to follow him; he would be glad to have him out of the way. Grimly, the boy dug his heels into his mount's flanks and urged him into a smooth trot.

Dawn was only a few faint whisps of light on the eastern horizon when he rode into town, dismounted, and tied his horse to the hitching post. He was waiting on the front steps of the general store when Roy Ingerton came across the dusty street a few minutes before seven.

"John Breckenridge," he exclaimed. "Whatever are you doing here?"

This was the moment John had feared the most. Ingerton and Waddy were good friends. He wondered how much the storekeeper would suspect and what he would say or do.

"I need some grub," John answered, trying to sound casual and unconcerned. "And I need some shells for my rifle and six-gun."

Ingerton pushed past him, the wooden steps creaking under his ponderous frame, and inserted the key in the heavy lock. "Been waiting long?"

"Not very."

"You must've got up mighty early. It's a far piece out to the Rocking Seven."

"Sort of."

"Waddy send you?" Ingerton asked.

John eyed him narrowly. He felt like telling the nosy storekeeper that it was none of his business. John was spending cash money and it shouldn't make any difference whether his stepfather had sent him or not. But he knew he had to give an answer that satisfied the storekeeper or he might not get the supplies he needed.

"Waddy's a-going to take me hunting," he said. "I couldn't sleep so I thought I'd ride in and save us some time."

That seemed to satisfy Ingerton. "I remember how excited I was when my pa took me on my first hunting expedition. Hardly closed my eyes all night for fear he'd go off and leave me."

The boy gave him the order and Ingerton

stared at the items, questions lurking in his squinting eyes.

"Must be quite a hunting trip."

"We was almost out of some stuff."

Ingerton pursed his lips as though he was about to protest. In that moment John remembered that Waddy had been in only the week before and had stocked their pantry for several months. Suspicion gleamed in the storekeeper's dark features but he said no more as he filled the list, setting the items on the rough, well-worn counter.

"That will be $9.38," he said when he finished adding up the purchases.

John's hands trembled as he counted out the money.

"Thank you," Ingerton said when the boy had paid him. "And tell Waddy hello for me."

John's cheeks crimsoned. "I'll do that."

He was at the door with his purchases when Ingerton stopped him. "If I was you," the storekeeper said evenly, "I'd take that six-gun off till I learned to use it. Anyone who sees that weapon on your belly might think you're an old hand with it. It could get you into a peck of trouble."

John realized he hadn't deceived the storekeeper after all. Ingerton knew what he was about. Hurriedly, he left the store, tied his grub stake to the back of his saddle with the bedroll, and mounted to ride off. He forced Rusty into a brisk trot and kept him moving until they were out of town. He had debated going west toward Laramie where he could lie about his age and join the army, but he had also thought about going east to Abilene where he could get a job pushing cattle north from Texas to the railhead. At the fork he had to make a decision, even if he changed his mind later. He had to choose one route or the other and keep moving. Pulling in a deep breath he turned east along the dusty, deep-rutted trail.

Back in Weaverville, Ingerton took off his apron, saddled his horse and rode out to the Rocking Seven to tell Waddy about John. The burly rancher dropped heavily into a kitchen chair and rested his arms on the table in front of him.

"I knew it," he murmured. "He's been acting strange for the last few days. When I got up this morning and found him gone I knew what he'd done."

Miriam started to cry and Waddy tried hard to comfort her, but Fletcher made no effort to conceal his satisfaction. "You ain't going after him, are you, Pa?"

Waddy shook his head. "Ain't no use. We'd just as well let him go. If he don't want to stay, he'll just take off another time when he gets the chance."

Ingerton understood. "I'm sorry, Waddy. I'd have stopped him if I could've."

The rancher looked up. "I don't blame you, but I've come to be mighty fond of that boy. He was another son to me. . . . I'm a-going to miss him, that's for sure."

4

John swayed rhythmically in the saddle as the big sorrel paced without effort across the barren wastes of Wyoming Territory in the direction of the bluestem country of Nebraska Territory. For two endless, wearing days he had faced the relentless blast of the scorching midsummer wind that swept across the grassland. It dried up the sweat on his lean, dirt-streaked cheeks as fast as it formed and whipped the moisture from his lips, leaving them seared and cracked.

The buffalo grass that covered much of the prairie was born to adversity. Tough and wiry as cacti, it battled savagely against the soaring temperatures and continuing lack of rain. However, it was finally overwhelmed by the persistence of the drought. The pale green of earlier, more pleasant days, faded in the extreme heat, becoming tinder-dry under foot and charred brown, lifeless as tumbleweed. And so it slept until the rains would come to coax life up from the dormant roots. But that was weeks away and for now the land was a desert.

Yucca, with its spiny plumes reaching upward and out in forbidding clusters, tried hard to provide a touch of green to the winterlike hues around the horse and rider. There was no food value in the various forms of cacti on either side of the trail, and the sage that seemed little affected by the lack of moisture was fibrous and leathery. Even the rail-thin antelope scorned such stubborn, scrubby plants. A pair of dust devils swirled wildly across the empty creek bed that paralleled the trail and danced to some frantic inner tune as they darted one direction and another over the endless prairies.

John wiped at his grimy face with a weary hand and pulled the neckerchief at his throat over his mouth and nostrils. He grasped the saddle horn and twisted to glance up at the sun. In a few hours it would be setting and the searing heat would begin to moderate, making the ride a bit more bearable for both himself and his horse.

If it had not been for the urgency that had sent him away from the Rocking Seven he would have turned and retraced his steps. Anything at the ranch would be better than this. Anything at all. Yet, he had been forced to leave. He had to keep moving, pressing toward the streams and water holes he hoped were just ahead.

He planned to stop at the end of two days to allow Rusty to rest and feed, but he could not. The water holes and streams he had been depending upon had disappeared and he didn't know how far he would have to ride to find more. The Platte River lay to the south, somewhere beyond the shimmering waves of heat that seemed to move skyward, short of the horizon. He had never seen the Platte, but Waddy talked about it often; a wide, shallow stream with a deceptively strong current. According to his stepfather, the Platte was an unfailing source of water.

John disliked going out of his way, but both

he and the horse had to have water and soon. That savage, pounding heat would take its toll if he didn't find water for them. He turned the big sorrel and headed across the prairies southward toward the Platte. The gelding's head came up in a quick, defiant gesture and he stepped out briskly.

When the sun was down and the shadows merged one into another, John stopped in a narrow ravine. He unsaddled his horse and hobbled him. Then, using his hat as a pail, he poured a little water into it from his canteen to give the sorrel a drink. It was not enough to satisfy the horse's thirst, but sharing it made him feel better.

Before dipping into his supplies for a meal, he gathered buffalo chips and was about to start a fire when he heard the haunting cry of an owl. He stopped quickly and reached for the Sharps a scant arm's length away, listening intently for the cry to come again. His first thought was that a band of Sioux had seen him and his horse in the dim light and were moving stealthily toward him. A horse like Rusty was enough to attract the attention of anyone who rode.

The cry came a second time and he relaxed slightly. It had not echoed in the stillness of the night; it had been made by a bird and not a man. Yet though he was certain the owl's hooting had not been the work of another human, he did not lessen his vigilance immediately. Without taking time to eat, he made a wide, meandering circle around the campsite, proving to himself that there was no one else nearby.

When John was satisfied that he was alone he returned to the camp. He decided against building a fire, just as an added precaution. He didn't want to carelessly draw attention to himself. He ate hardtack and a piece of jerky and stretched out in his blankets to get some sleep. Once more he began to wish that he had stayed at the Rocking Seven. Even putting up with Fletch was better than this. At least while he was with Waddy he had a good bed and three big meals a day and plenty of oats and grass and water for Rusty. But exhaustion soon crowded out his troubles and moments later he was asleep.

When he awakened, the sun was high and a scorching summer wind seared his face. He came alive slowly, blinking against the harsh rays of light. Gradually, however, his senses returned. He pulled himself slowly to a sitting position and stared at the terrain around him.

Rusty!

Fear tightened its clammy hands on his stomach. His horse was gone; someone had stolen him! Hurriedly he groped for his boots and the six-gun he had taken off and put under the saddle he used as a pillow. He pulled on the boots and strapped the heavy Colt to his waist. Then, the Sharps at the ready, he started forward, studying the tracks that led out of the ravine toward the crest of a small hill. His senses were alert to every sound, every movement.

It was strange that whoever stole his horse hadn't taken his weapon or the grub or the leather pouch he kept his money in. Yet, he had to be cautious—more cautious than he had ever been. It was like Waddy always said: Anyone who would take a man's horse and leave him on foot in desolate country would stop at nothing.

John examined the ground carefully. He saw the marks of shod hooves in the grass. That would be Rusty. But he could not find any sign of another horse. That would indicate the thief had approached on foot. But, if he had, where had he come from and where had he been? Or had the boy missed the footprints of another animal?

He went back over the area alert and wary, the way Waddy had taught him to track. Rusty's trail was as plain as the path from Weaverville to the Rocking Seven, but, studying the ground as he would, he could find no sign of another horse accompanying his mount.

He followed Rusty's trail to the crest of the hill. Rusty had not been grazing; he had moved in a straight line, as though he was being ridden or led. Yet, he was still wearing hobbles. His stride was short, an indication that the ropes were still in place. If someone had stolen the big horse, why wouldn't he have removed the restraints? Why leave them on and risk being seen during the time it would take to get the gelding away from the camp?

At the top of the grade John paused and looked about. Below him, at the foot of the steep incline, he saw a wide silver band winding among the trees, and lush grass on either side. It was a broad, placid river that seemed not to be in a hurry: a lazy stretch of water that found its way eastward among long, narrow bars of sand, dividing it into a number of channels. The Platte!

John hadn't realized he had traveled that far south, but there it was. And just as Waddy described it. He had never seen the river but he recognized it instantly. While he stared down at the scene before him he caught a flash of red among the green of the willows and cottonwood.

Rusty! He could see a patch of the gelding's

broad back. Relief surged through John. Now he knew exactly what had happened. Smelling water, his horse had made for the stream and the thick stand of grass. No one had stolen him.

Gratefully, John moved down the slope in the direction of the grazing horse. Rusty was still wearing the hobbles and the halter with its short hank of rope in the ring. Talking softly to him, John approached. Once or twice the animal moved away, but only a few feet before starting to graze again. In a moment the boy had the rope. He checked the hobbles to be certain they were still firmly in place and took Rusty deeper into the trees, so he wouldn't be spotted so easily if anyone came by. Then he moved his own gear down to the bank of the wide stream and made camp in a thick stand of cottonwood and brush along the bank. He snared a rabbit, skinned and roasted it over a tiny fire that sent a thin, almost transparent whisp of smoke toward the treetops where it was caught by the wind and dispersed. With satisfaction he noted that it could not be seen two hundred yards away. He hadn't come across anyone on the trail since leaving Weaverville, but there was no use taking chances. Waddy had taught him that. Leave a thin trail or no trail at all and constantly cover the rear so you won't be taken unawares.

John planned to wait until the following morning to hit the trail again. That would give Rusty a chance to rest and graze. This time, he decided, he would skirt the Platte on his way east. There was more chance of running into others on the trail along the river and he didn't look forward to that, but with the drought like it was he didn't want to take a chance of running out of water again.

Dawn crept from its resting place below the horizon the next morning. The eastern sky seemed to lighten slightly and after a time faint slivers of light showed through the thin, wispy clouds to mark the outer rim of the earth. John had been sleeping soundly but when the darkness began to disappear, he awakened, turned over in his bed-roll and sat up, scrubbing at his eyes.

Toward morning, just before waking up, he had dreamed about Ma and Miriam. He could see them framed in the doorway of the sprawling ranch house. He must have been out in the barn or at the well. Ma was motioning for him to join them. It took a minute or two to realize what she wanted, but when he started forward hesitantly, Ma and Miriam were suddenly whisked to the field behind the house. As he advanced they moved backward, smiling and beckoning him to follow. But, try as he would, he could not close the gap between himself and them.

He continued to be disturbed by the dream as he put on his hat, pulled on his boots, and went out to check on Rusty. He was still shaken by the scare of the day before when he was sure the big horse had been stolen. However, the sorrel gelding was still there, grazing not more than fifty feet from the place where he had been the night before. Satisfied that his mount was all right, Breckenridge went back to his camp, kindled the small fire, and cooked breakfast.

When he had crawled into his bedroll the night before he had been determined to get up and get on the trail shortly after daylight. Now, however, a certain lethargy took hold of him—a vague feeling of uneasiness that kept him from moving rapidly. He could still see his ma and sister standing in the doorway as they had in his dream. He had never known them to look more beautiful, more appealing. But he hadn't been able to get close to them. When he tried to reach them, they moved to the field, backwards, slowly, gliding farther and farther away as he struggled to approach them. The dream had been so real he felt completely rejected by them both.

Greatly disturbed, he fought against the empty aching in the pit of his stomach. He was hungry, yet he didn't feel much like eating. He knew, however, that he had to down a sizeable breakfast if he were to have strength for the day; it might be dark before he would have the opportunity to eat again.

He forced himself to eat a piece of ham and finish the pancakes. Then he wiped out the heavy cast-iron skillet and put out the fire. Once that was accomplished he got his bedroll and gear together and tied them behind the saddle. As he put one foot in the stirrup and lifted his head in order to mount the big horse, he caught sight of several twisting plumes of smoke reaching upward toward the western sky.

He started suddenly. He had been out that way the afternoon before and had seen nothing. That meant whoever was there had come in from the west, traveling the same direction he was.

His pulse quickened and he felt his cheeks flush as he settled into the saddle and shucked the Sharps from its scabbard. Indians! That was the only possibility that made sense! He moved forward cautiously, trying to sort out what was happening and decide what to do.

He couldn't stand and fight them. He was alone, and if those fires had been built by a war party, there could be seventy-five or a hundred Indians. But it couldn't be a war party. A tribe about to do battle would have built fires so clean and smokeless he would have had no thought that they were within a hundred miles. And they would have been on the move with the coming dawn. Whoever these people were, they were in no hurry.

Then he remembered: This was the time of year the plains Indians followed the buffalo herds to get their winter meat and hides for robes and tepees. The women and children would be along. That was the reason for being careless with their cooking fires. They were peaceful, so they saw no reason for hiding their presence in the area.

John started out to the trail, but thought about Rusty and changed his mind. He had seen cow-hands and drovers alike studying the big, power-fully built gelding as he rode down the broad street of Weaverville. The Indian braves would be the same. Letting them see the beautiful animal might cause them to get greedy and try to steal him. It would be better to keep Rusty out of sight until they were gone. He turned the big red horse abruptly and rode him into the thickest willows where he dismounted and tied him as securely as possible to a fallen log. Then he sat down to wait.

John expected the Indians to arrive in a short time, but it was almost noon before he saw the first faint puffs of dust stirred up by many feet. He crouched for half an hour in the brush near his horse while the noisy band approached on the trail just above the river. Then, curious, he left his hiding place, crawling on his stomach through the grass and brush, his rifle in one hand. In two or three minutes he reached a place where he could part the willows and look across the open prairie to the trail.

The older braves and leaders of the tribe were in the lead and had already passed John's hiding place by the time he reached it. Behind them came the younger braves, proud men with straight backs and lean, muscular arms. John expected to see a few rifles, but there were none. This hunting party would have to depend on their traditional bows and arrows.

Behind the young braves the women rode with their travoises loaded with tepees and cooking utensils and small children. The rest of the tribe followed: young women and boys and girls running noisily about at the rear of the procession. A few of the older boys lagged behind the motley procession playing some sort of game until the main group was far ahead. Then they scampered to catch up. And the dogs! There seemed to be a dozen scrawny, half-starved creatures, snarling and barking at each other and the boys who were playing.

Suddenly John realized the danger they presented. At any moment one of them could catch his scent and alert the braves with that peculiar bark indicating a stranger was about. That would be disastrous! Hurriedly he backed off, anxious to put as much space between himself and the Indians and their dogs as possible.

Once he was back where he had tied Rusty he relaxed. He could still hear the shouting and barking and see the powdered dust rising toward the cloudless sky, but there was no indication that he had been discovered.

John's original plan had been to ride in the same direction the Indians had been traveling, but he couldn't do that now. At least not right away. He would have to allow them time enough to locate the buffalo and move off the main-traveled route. Since they were hunting they would not be staying on the trail for long. If he had patience they would be out of his way.

It was not easy to wait in the trees along the river. He was anxious to be on the way again, to get to Abilene and try to find a job as a drover for the coming year. It was too late now to catch a herd going north, so there was no use in even thinking about going down into Texas; the herds were already on their way. Maybe he could find a trail boss who had finished his drive to the rail-head and was about to head for home—someone who would hire him for the winter at little more than meals and a place to stay so he could help with the drive the following spring. If he couldn't get a job like that he would find something as a hostler in a livery barn or as a dishwasher in a café or sweeping out a store and stocking shelves. Anything to earn a little money. One thing about Waddy Ross, he had taught him to work.

Yet, anxious as he was to keep moving, he knew it was best to wait at least until after sundown. He went down to the place where Rusty was grazing and watched him from the shade of a stately broad-leafed cottonwood. Toward afternoon he dozed for a couple of hours. He would be riding most of the night; it was best that both he and his mount had some extra rest.

As the sun went down the savage heat moderated. By this time the Indians had made camp a short distance east of his hiding place. Within the hour he had seen new plumes of smoke that indicated the band had stopped and the women were making camp and fixing supper. He would ride north, putting miles between himself and the Indian camp before turning east to pass them. Such caution might not be necessary but it was better to be careful than to have your scalp on some Indian's belt. That was what Waddy always said.

He caught Rusty and led him out of the thick stand of willows and cottonwood. He had a foot in the stirrup and was about to swing himself onto the sorrel gelding when a shrill, nerve-shattering yell exploded upon him! An Indian hunting party charged his direction from a stand of trees, arrows nocked and bows drawn.

Rusty reared in terror and before the battle cry reached its apex, an arrow seared John's shoulder, ripping his shirt. The distance closed as the exultant young braves dashed in for the kill. Rusty's sudden lunge threw John off to one side just enough to save his life. A second arrow whistled past, a hair's width from his neck, thudding into the cantle of his pa's old saddle.

The big horse bolted as the braves swept by and one grasped desperately for his bridle. John clawed the Colt from its holster and dashed for the cover of the nearest trees. They saw what he was intending to do and stormed back, screams of triumph filling the still early evening air. They were young and reckless, unseasoned in battle, but eager to show their bravery so they could boast around the campfires.

John made it to a clump of spindling willows that offered no protection save the partial screening of his slight figure and waited for the murderous braves to storm within range of his six-gun. They were a scant eighty yards away when a yell behind him shrilled above the others. Instinctively he threw himself to the ground, rolled over and lifted the heavy Peacemaker.

A lone Indian who must have hung back when the others launched the first attack charged in from the opposite direction, certain now that he would perform the coup and have the privilege of lifting John's scalp. His tomahawk raised for the kill, he leaned forward on his hard-running pony when John squeezed the trigger. The deadly axe started downward but didn't finish the swing. The warrior's grip relaxed and the weapon slipped from his fingers, clattering harmlessly to the ground. The war cry died on the young Indian's lips, choked by an involuntary scream of terror as he toppled from the back of his speeding mount, rolled in the grass, and was still.

Another brave, closer than his companions, thundered towards John, his bow at full draw. John sensed what was happening and spun to fire without aiming. The bullet hit the brave's forearm, shattering the bone. He dropped the bow, threw his arms in the air, and slid from the back of his wiry pinto into the path of the pounding hooves of the horse behind him. The animal stumbled over the lithe, half-naked figure and fell, throwing his rider.

The Indian scrambled to his feet, tearing a knife from his belt as though he was about to charge young Breckenridge. But he didn't have time to make his move. John's bullet caught him in the chest. He straightened slowly, stupidly, and tried to speak, but the words only rattled in his throat. He fell forward and remained motionless.

The ferocity of John's counterattack stunned the rest of the attacking party and they whirled and galloped out of range. There had been five in the group that he knew of and he had accounted for three of those, but he was sure there were others lurking in the shadows, waiting to press the attack. It was his first Indian fight but he knew it wasn't over. There would be a brief respite while they regrouped and planned how to assault him. If they needed reinforcements a courier would be sent to the band for help.

He took this opportunity to wriggle backward through the grass to the partial safety of the trees. Sweat pearled his face and his hands trembled as he realized the seriousness of the situation.

5

In spite of the terror that gripped the big sorrel, Rusty had raced into the trees a hundred yards and stopped. The skin on his withers quivered violently, his nostrils flared and his eyes were wide and rolling.

John crept stealthily toward him, talking softly in an effort to reassure the frightened animal. The gelding jerked his head and moved a few feet away. "There now, Rusty," he crooned. "Easy, boy. Easy."

The second try he was able to get close enough to catch the dangling rein with his hand. He made his way along the horse's powerful neck and shucked the rifle from the scabbard. He only had a brief time before the attack would begin again, but it was imperative that he get Rusty securely tied. If his horse was frightened off or taken by the Indians he might just as well be killed himself. There would be no way out.

Hurriedly he removed the bridle, put the halter on his saddle horse and tied him securely in the thickest stand of willows nearby. Then, several yards away he scrunched behind some fallen logs, wedging himself in as much as possible to avoid being seen easily and to protect himself from the Indians' arrows. With the safety off on the Sharps he waited tensely for the next attack.

At first John felt he had found a safe position among the fallen cottonwoods, but now he realized it hadn't been a good idea. He had to be in a spot where he could face an assault from any direction. He had to be able to move quickly to keep the attackers from pinpointing his exact location by the sounds of his rifle. He pulled himself out of the narrow wedge between the logs and chose instead a clump of cottonwoods thick enough to deflect their arrows and, at least partially, screen him from view.

He waited silently peering into the brush around him for some sign that his attackers had moved close to him—a slight movement of the grass and twigs, the muffled sound of footsteps, whisper-soft, or the glimpse of a dark shape hugging the ground. His eyes were never still as he searched the trees and his ears were finely tuned to the faintest of sounds.

The next move of his assailants was not long in coming. He had been looking and listening for evidence that the Indians were drawing the net tighter about him, but the first sound came from some distance away, the faint, lilting cry of a whippoorwill. It echoed weakly through the trees to his right and the hair on the back of his neck raised: That was no bird! Only the human voice echoed that way.

As the first notes died the answering call came from somewhere behind him. That one was closer—much closer! He spun quickly and fired in the direction of the cry. There was no real chance of hitting one of them, shooting blind, but it might help to keep them off balance and make them a bit more cautious about moving in.

In an hour it would be dark and with the

coming of darkness the chances were that the attack would cease until morning. According to what Waddy Ross had told him, Indians didn't like to attack at night. But that didn't mean the siege would end. They would be out there in the night, probably with reinforcements brought over from their camp to keep him from slipping away. And with the coming of dawn they would move in on him again.

The silence that followed his last shot was disconcerting. It seemed to spread over the trees and the river until even the wind was hushed and still. A strange, unnatural quiet reigned—a quiet that was both solemn and ominous.

John wriggled to a spot about twenty feet away and squeezed off three rounds. He was in the process of moving once more, trying to make his attackers think there were several pinned down in the trees along the river instead of one lone, frightened boy. At that moment a volley of shots from outside the trees greeted him. At first he was certain an Indian with a rifle had joined the battle, but the shooting was followed by a piercing, triumphant Johnny Reb yell, "Yahoo!"

John put a hand along his mouth and raised to his knees. "Yahoo!" he cried in the wild, exuberant shout of southern soldiers in battle, "Yahoo!"

The shooting began again, indiscriminate firing that stopped only when the rifle was empty. John knew what he had to do! The firing from outside the trees would bewilder the braves momentarily. They would have to stop closing in on their intended victim and endeavor to wipe out this new threat. The chance for him to get away wouldn't last long, perhaps only a few brief seconds. He had to break out of the ambush while their attention was diverted.

Hurriedly, he scrambled to his feet and dashed for the place where his horse was tethered. He jerked the reins free and leaped into the saddle. Then, bending low over Rusty's neck, he kicked him in the flanks and the big sorrel burst out of the trees at top speed. As the stranger heard the horse's frantic plunging through the brush he opened up again from somewhere behind John on the other side of the narrow band of trees, firing six times in rapid succession.

John skirted the trees along the river for half a mile or more. The big sorrel was running flat out, his powerful hooves pounding the virgin prairie. Finally, in the growing darkness young Breckenridge reigned in slightly and glanced over his shoulder. A lone rider was following. He wasn't far behind, but the dusk was so near upon them the boy could barely see the shape of the horse and rider. Yet he knew that the one following was his benefactor. The man was riding a big horse for one thing; far bigger than the little ponies most of the Indians used. And he sat his mount like one in a saddle while the braves rode bareback. It had to be the man who had saved his life. John reigned in and waited.

Moments later the stranger joined him. He was a slight, lean-faced individual with features leathered by the sun and wind. His rifle was still across the pommel of his well-worn Texas saddle, the thin fingers on his right hand clutching it firmly above the stock.

"Howdy, Mister," young Breckenridge said. "I'm right thankful for your help. I was plumb scared I was going to wind up without my hair."

The rider on the big bay laughed shortly. "When I heard the shooting and seen them Indian ponies down by the trees I figgered they sure enough had an old she-bear cornered. I didn't know it was a cub!"

The boy bristled and his hand moved down to the butt of his six-gun, calling attention to its presence. "I'm old enough to take care of myself," he retorted.

The stranger nodded. "You were doing a right good job back there!" He stood in the stirrups and turned to look back in the direction from which they had come.

In the few moments they had been talking night descended upon them. The sun had long since set in the west but the darkening sky was still lighter than the woods. The trees loomed a great, shapeless mass along the river, a shroud so thick and black it would effectively screen the approach of the braves if they decided to give chase. Still, there was no sound to break the hush that engulfed them, no indication that the Indians were in pursuit.

"We'd better get a move on," the man said. "I don't reckon we'll be followed, dark as it is, but you never can tell." They rode off at a brisk canter.

By this time John was beginning to realize all that had happened. Until that moment, the brief, violent battle with the Indians had seemed more like a dream—a nightmare that had happened only in his fitful sleep or tortured imagination. Now he knew it was all too true. If it hadn't been for the stranger who rode at his side he would probably have lost his life. His hand trembled on the saddle horn and he glanced quickly at his companion to see if he had noticed. By this time, however, it was too dark to see much of anything.

"I don't think they're coming after us," the man said. "Leastwise, not tonight. And by morning we'll be far enough away so's it won't make no difference."

John relaxed. "That's good news."

"By the way," the stranger said, as though he had just thought of it, "I don't even know your name."

"John."

"Got another handle to go with that one?"

"Yeah. My name's Breckenridge. John Breckenridge."

His companion jerked the bay to a stop. "I've only met one other man by the name of Breckenridge in my whole life. Feller by the name of George."

John was aware that his companion was staring at him, though he could only see the outline of his features. "He was my pa."

"If that don't beat the cards! I rode with George Breckenridge once a long time ago. It wasn't for long but I got to know him well enough to know he was a man. A real, honest to goodness man." Impulsively he held out his hand. "I want to shake hands with you, Kid Breckenridge. My name's Corbitt. Lee Corbitt. That pa of yours was something!"

They rode on, making their way along the river in the darkness, trying to put as many miles between them and the Indians as possible. For the first two or three hours clouds scurried across the sky, keeping the countryside in stygian blackness. About midnight, however, the heavens cleared and the soft silver sheen of moon lighted the way.

Young Breckenridge and Corbitt had been plodding forward in silence, each wrapped in his own thoughts. But the dim light seemed to loosen their tongues. They began to talk.

Corbitt didn't question John directly about his reasons for leaving home. That wasn't the way of the hard-faced men who roamed the frontier. A man's past was his own business. He gave his correct name or another, as it suited him, and no one dared question him as to who he was or what he had been. Desperadoes and law-abiding men mingled freely, accepted for what they said they were until circumstances proved otherwise.

But the older rider got John to talking and soon the whole story was out.

"Ever think you shoulda talked to Waddy first?" Corbitt asked. "So's you'd know for sure he didn't want you? . . . You mighta made a mistake about that."

Breckenridge shook his head. "I didn't make no mistake! He wanted to get rid of me, so I skinned out! I wasn't staying where I wasn't wanted."

Corbitt rode on for several minutes without speaking. Then he turned to his young companion. "You sure handled yourself proud back there. How old are you, anyway?"

"Getting close to seventeen."

The corners of Lee Corbitt's mouth tightened. "That's a good age. A right good age."

"What do ya mean by that?"

"You're old enough to learn and young enough to teach. It's a good age." He fell silent for a time. "I think I was about your age when Pa got me a six-gun and taught me to use it."

John pulled the Colt Peacemaker from its

holster and hefted it proudly. "I've already got me a gun," he said. "It was Pa's. Just as soon as I get somewhere so I can get me a job and buy ammunition, I'm going to start practicing with it."

"You've got a right good weapon there," Corbitt said. "Your pa wouldn't have nothing less than the best. But don't you think it's a mite heavy for you?"

The boy's cheeks darkened. "I'll manage."

Corbitt stood in the stirrups and looked back toward the coming dawn. "You've got to remember: Your life might be on the line some day and the weight of that old hog nose can be just enough to slow you so the other guy'll get the jump. It could be your life, kid."

Young Breckenridge hesitated, thinking over the matter somberly. "It was good enough for Pa. It'll be good enough for me!"

"Your pa was big and he was a growed man! I'll bet he didn't start out with no Peacemaker. What you need is a lighter weapon to start on. You can learn with a Smith and Wesson .32 and use it till you're big enough to handle your pa's. Believe me, kid, I know. And if your pa was here, he'd tell you the same thing."

"Only I ain't got no money to buy another gun!" he blurted desperately.

Corbitt grinned. "I think maybe I can fix you up."

John's expression did not change. "I ain't got no money and I ain't got a job. Not yet, I ain't. I couldn't pay you back so I can't be beholden to you any more'n I am already."

"Who knows?" Corbitt said. "Maybe you can work for me."

Hope gleamed in the boy's features. "I'm sure a-looking for a job. What would I be doing if I worked for you?"

His companion's expression changed slightly. An icy curtain dropped over his pale blue eyes, clouding any manifestation of emotion. Then he laughed. "I'll think of something."

After a minute or more he spoke again. "Right now I've got a gun in my saddlebags that's just about like you'll need, along with a couple of boxes of cartridges. A friend of mine got his self killed over North Platte way a couple of weeks ago. I told the marshal I'd take his stuff to his widow and tell her what happened. . . . She ain't going to care if you use it, at least for awhile."

"I'll think on it," the boy said, reluctantly. Somehow he felt as though he would be disloyal to his pa for even considering another weapon. Still, Corbitt sounded as though he knew what he was talking about. And it was like Waddy said, when you met a man who was an expert you listened to what he had to say. "I'll think on it."

"You do that," his companion answered.

After a time, when the sun was poking its head over the horizon and the wind promised to sweep the prairie with its scorching breath, Corbitt suggested they go into the trees along the river to get a little sleep and allow their mounts to rest and graze.

"We've got a long, dry ride ahead of us to the Republican River."

"Think we need to stand guard?" John asked. He had never been out on the trail when anyone stood guard, except when they were driving cattle, but he had heard his stepfather talk about it. It sounded like the wise thing to do in Indian country.

"Not this time," Corbitt replied. "If that little hunting party was really on our tail they'd be here by now."

So they put out their bedrolls and lay down, heads pillowed in their saddles. John was certain he would not be able to sleep at all after everything that had happened the last few hours. But he closed his eyes and the next thing he knew Corbitt was shaking him. "Time to move!"

John sat up, blinking stupidly in the brilliant sunlight. For a moment he thought he was back home and Waddy or Fletch was getting him up to help with the chores. As his eyes focused, however, he realized he was on the trail with a stranger.

He crawled out quickly, caught up Rusty and saddled him. A few hundred yards beyond the place where they had slept, they forded the shallow, swift-moving Platte and headed into the rough terrain between the two rivers. The hills stretched endlessly in every direction; they were completely devoid of trees and barren, save for the sun-blistered buffalo grass and an occasional clump of Spanish Sword or cacti. This was buffalo grazing land. The chips that marked their passing this way were everywhere.

"Any danger of running into Indians?" John asked, trying to sound casual and unconcerned.

"There's always a chance of running into a band of renegades," Corbitt admitted, "but it ain't likely. The buffalo have moved on and about the only game around here are a few antelopes and rabbits and prairie dogs. The hunting parties ain't going to spend no time around here."

When they finally reached the smaller of the two rivers—the narrow, muddy Republican —Corbitt turned west. They continued in that direction until they reached a two-room dugout with stubby sod walls on the exposed sides and across the front. A sod roof completed the structure. The exposed portion of the strange dwelling sagged wearily on one corner and the heavy wooden door looked as though it had not been opened in years. A short distance in front of the dugout stood a pole-fenced corral that appeared to have outlived its usefulness. The sticks for the fence had been chosen carelessly and had been even more carelessly stuck into the ground. They leaned in all directions, and along one side twenty feet of the fence was gone altogether. A makeshift gate on the side facing the dugout completed the enclosure.

John's eyes widened. "We going to stay here?"

"For awhile."

The boy dismounted and looked around. "Is this place yours?" he asked, incredulously.

"Not exactly. I found it a couple of years ago and have been coming back here from time to time ever since."

Young Breckenridge went over to the door and pushed. It squealed and groaned, but opened.

"Don't go in yet," Corbitt warned. "We've gotta check for rattlesnakes first."

John shuddered.

Corbitt searched the abandoned dugout carefully. There was no sign of rattlesnakes or even the more numerous bull snakes.

"We're in luck," he said, jerking the gear off the back of his big bay and carrying it inside. "It's July and they've all moved out for the summer. Come here in the fall when they're starting to den or April when it begins to warm up and it'll be a different story."

John wasn't sure he wanted to sleep in the dugout. He would feel much better under the scraggly, half-dead trees, but he couldn't let Corbitt know that. He had dozens of questions to ask his companion, but there was a firmness in the older man's manner that choked them off, unspoken. Nothing more was said about his staying with Corbitt. The stranger just assumed that was the way it should be and John went along with it.

The boy wanted to know why they were stopping on such a desolate stretch of the river. It hadn't been chance that brought them to the dugout. Corbitt had sought it out, deliberately. It was probably where he had been heading when he heard the shooting and came to John's rescue. He also wanted to know about the job that had been offered. What it paid didn't matter so much as long as he got a little money for clothes and things like shells. What he really was wondering was what he would be doing and where they would live.

Maybe Corbitt had a ranch somewhere. He might have left it temporarily to drive cattle up to Wyoming or Montana, and was now on his way home. But, if that were true, he wouldn't be stopping in an abandoned dugout and he wouldn't be traveling alone. If he had been taking a herd north, he would surely have a couple of his regular hands with him. Most of the drovers would have been paid off at their destination, but he would have had at least two men along that he could depend on. There was a certain mystery about Corbitt, but he wasn't the kind John could question.

The following morning the older man dug a .32 caliber Smith and Wesson from his saddlebags and gave it to Breckenridge, along with two boxes of shells. "Try this," he said. "I think it'll be a lot better for you—at least 'til you fill out some. . . . Notice how much lighter it is in your hand."

John had to admit that was true. "I'll try it," he said after a time. "But if it don't work for me like you say, I'm a-going back to Pa's Colt."

For the next two weeks they camped on the river, hunting for food to add to the staples Corbitt had cached in the dugout some time before. They killed two antelope and five speedy, long-eared jacks for meat and caught a few fish. It was a tiresome diet but at least they weren't going hungry.

Corbitt worked tirelessly with young Breckenridge, teaching him to use the handgun. He showed him how to wear the holster so it would permit him to whip the weapon free and shoot in the quickest possible time. There weren't enough cartridges to practice as much as John would have liked so Corbitt had him working with an empty gun at first. The older man insisted that he keep practicing until he knew how to draw and aim instinctively before he allowed him to fire the weapon. It became more exciting after that. He was faster than he ever hoped he would be and as accurate as though he had been shooting for twenty years. It wasn't long until Corbitt could throw a buffalo chip into the air and the boy would drill a hole in it before it touched the ground.

"Just as I thought," his teacher said. "You'll make a gunman like your pa or I'll miss my guess."

John flushed with pride. From that moment on his teaching changed abruptly.

"I'm goin' to tell you a secret I ain't never told nobody," Corbitt said. "I don't know whether it'll work for you, but it sure has worked for me.

If you get the hang of it, there won't be no one nowhere as can beat you."

"Great!"

"You've got to promise me one thing or I'll keep it to myself. You've got to promise that you'll work harder than you've ever worked at anything before. You've got to be willing to practice at least two hours every day."

"Where'll I get the cartridges?"

"You won't need many. You can practice without shooting." He lowered his voice as though he feared being overheard. "You've got to think of your gun as an extension of your hand—your fingers. As fast as you can move your hand you can move that gun." He held out his hand with his gun in it. "I don't *think* about pulling my weapon. I don't *think* about shooting. I don't think about nothing but getting my hand up as quick as I can." He showed John how quick he was at the draw.

The boy gasped.

"You can do the same, if you work at it."

Young Breckenridge went back to his practicing with renewed vigor. He kept telling himself that the gun was a part of his hand—an extension of his fingers. All he had to do was jerk his hand up and point it. Gradually, he felt himself getting faster. And with the speed came a new confidence. He was going to be able to handle a gun like his pa. Maybe not as fast, but fast enough. Plenty fast enough.

6

They had been at the dugout for more than two weeks when John saw a certain restlessness develop in his companion: an impatience that grew with each passing day. Corbitt was up earlier than usual and couldn't remain still for long. He was constantly on the move, making his way to the top of the low bluffs along the south side of the river and staring out over the scorched prairie as though he were expecting visitors. On other occasions he went to the edge of the murky water and studied the narrow, twisting stream.

"Expecting somebody?" John asked.

The instant he spoke he knew he shouldn't have. Anger flecked Corbitt's pale eyes and the muscles in his neck tightened. "What business is that of yours?"

"None, I guess."

"Then keep your mouth shut."

That afternoon Corbitt surprised his young friend by going out to the old corral, looking at the fence for several minutes, and setting to work. He cut a number of cottonwood poles, hewed them to the proper length and set them in the ground.

John went out to help him.

"Cut some small poles," Corbitt told him.

Toward the middle of the afternoon Corbitt stopped for a cup of coffee. "I suppose you're a-wondering why I've decided to fix this fence?" he asked suddenly.

John hesitated. He was surprised at the flurry of activity and that it was directed toward re-building the corral. If Corbitt had started working on the roof of the sorry little dugout, or re-hung the only door, he would have understood. But that fence! It wasn't good for anything!

"I figgered you'd tell me if you wanted me to know."

His friend nodded approvingly. "Thought I'd start on it to have something to do," he explained. "And so the next guys who stop here'll have a place to keep their horses."

John raised his gaze to meet Corbitt's. "Ain't we going to leave before long?"

"We'll be moving on one of these days, don't worry about that. And when we do, you'll get plenty of riding." With that he finished his coffee and got to his feet. "Let's get back to it. Maybe we can finish before dark."

That statement disturbed John, too. If Corbitt was only fixing the corral to give them something to occupy their time, why would he be concerned about finishing the job that day?

The fence wasn't finished by supper time and when they had finished eating Corbitt told his young companion he had decided to wait until the next day to complete the task. "It won't take me more'n a couple of hours."

John's eyes narrowed. "What do you want *me* to do?"

Corbitt went to the old cookstove and poured himself another cup of scalding black coffee. "We're gettin' about out of grub," he said. "I think I'll have you go in to Gladstone tomorrow to get what we need."

"Gladstone?" John echoed. "Where's that?"

"Didn't I tell you? It's fifteen miles or so west of here. I'll give you a list of supplies to get and you can have my horse shod."

It seemed strange to John that Corbitt didn't insist on taking his own horse to the blacksmith. Waddy Ross was so particular about that job he wanted to be there so he could be sure it was done right. But young Breckenridge guessed that different guys had different ideas about horses and taking care of them.

The next morning he had breakfast shortly after daylight and went out to saddle his companion's big bay. He had never ridden the animal before but Corbitt didn't think he would have any problems.

"He's got a lot of vinegar, but you sit a horse well. You'll manage."

John put his left hand on the saddle horn and swung aboard. He felt the dark skin tremble beneath his knees and the bay's ears twitched nervously, but John was able to steady him.

"Now, remember," Corbitt continued, "drop the saddlebags off at McKenzie's Gun Shop on your way to the blacksmith's. When you've left the horse with Big Ed take the list over to the general store and have them fill it. There's money enough in this pouch to pay for everything."

John asked again about the road to Gladstone and was about to leave when Corbitt stopped him.

"Take that gun off!" he ordered.

"But I *always* wear it."

"Not this time. There're guys around Gladstone who'd look on that six-gun like a longhorn bull on the prod sees a red flag. They'd be aching to get at you to add another notch to their guns."

"I ain't got into trouble before," he said.

"Maybe you ain't, but you'll have a sight better chance of staying out of trouble iffen you leave it here."

Reluctantly, John undid the gun belt and handed it to his companion before riding off. He forded the river at the place he and Corbitt had crossed on their way to the Republican River and made his way north until he reached the east-west road that led to the stark little western community. Once on the trail he headed across the rolling prairie.

Corbitt's horse was a fine animal, but he wasn't Rusty. John didn't think there was another saddle horse in all of Nebraska Territory the equal of the powerful sorrel Waddy had given him. But the bay had a comfortable, tireless gait that ate up the miles.

John had never been in Gladstone. In fact he hadn't even known it existed until Corbitt told him the night before, but as he rode down the almost empty street he had the feeling he had visited there dozens of times. It was a typical western town with a series of stark, shabby buildings lining either side of the dusty road.

The Palace Hotel, an imposing two-story structure with broad windows along the front, introduced the business section of the community. It was the newest building in town and still boasted a gleaming coat of paint and a freshly decorated sign. Next door stood the Elite Barber Shop and the Cattlemen's Saloon, which was second only to the hotel in size. It was a squat, broad-beamed building with a faded sign across the front and listing, swinging doors. On the other side of the wide thoroughfare Esau's General Store beckoned the trade. Next to it two vacant lots were grown up to weeds made brown by the drought, and close against them was McKenzie's Gun Shop, a tired frame structure that gave every evidence of being about to collapse. The blacksmith's shop was located just beyond the bank.

John stopped in front of the gun shop, tied his mount to the hitching rail, and went inside with the saddlebags. "Corbitt said for me to bring these to you. There's a note inside."

The portly gunsmith lifted himself ponderously from his chair and waddled to the counter. He leaned heavily on it and peered down at the boy.

"Corbitt?" he echoed as though he had never heard of anyone by that name. "Corbitt? Do you mean *Lee* Corbitt?"

"That's right. I brought his horse in to get him shod an' pick up a few things. . . . I'm riding with him these days."

"Lee Corbitt," McKenzie repeated as though John's words had suddenly taken on meaning. "Why didn't you say so?" He reached for the saddlebags. "Come, come, lad. Give them to me."

He opened the flap and took out the note, adjusting his little round glasses on his nose in an effort to make out the faint, penciled writing better. "A Smith and Wesson .32," he mumbled. "Six boxes of .45 shells and three boxes of. . . ." His voice trailed off. "I'll get these things ready," he said after another moment. "Come back when you're going to leave town. They'll be ready."

John nodded. "Did you say there was a six-gun on that list?"

The gunsmith's black eyes slitted in his lumpish face. "Suppose you wait to find out what's in them saddlebags till you get them back to Corbitt. OK?"

John backed toward the door.

"And don't you tell him I said nothing. Y'hear?"

Without replying the boy went out into the rising morning heat and closed the door behind him. He couldn't figure out why old McKenzie was so touchy about that gun. Although John had forgotten it until that moment, Corbitt had talked with him several times about buying a gun and had him working with the Smith and Wesson that had belonged to his partner before he got shot. It wouldn't make any difference whether John told him what McKenzie had said or not. The question that bothered him the most was what he should do about taking it.

He wasn't going to be beholden to Corbitt any more than he already was. Of course his friend had talked about having him work. If he could pay for the gun that would change everything. Only working for Corbitt didn't make a lot of sense—at least so far. He didn't seem to have anything to do. For more than two weeks Corbitt hadn't asked him to do anything except work on that fence and make the trip into town. He never would earn enough to pay for the gun and holster that way.

John went to the blacksmith shop and then over to the general store with the list of supplies Corbitt wanted. From there he made his way to the post office. Corbitt had been most specific when he told John what he was to do when he got there.

"When you get to the post office," he said, "you'll find a window to the right of the door with

72

a glass broken out. There's a wooden box on a table in front of the window with some letters in it. Reach through the opening and check the letters to see if there're any there for Lefty Corban or C. Isaac Lee. If you find any addressed that way, bring them to me. OK?''

John's face had crinkled, questions gleaming in his eyes. There was no doubt but the letters for Lefty Corban were meant for his friend. But what about C. Isaac Lee? Who was that? When Waddy or his ma had gotten mail their names were spelled right out on the envelope, plain as could be.

And why use a box the men went through to pick out their own mail? Why didn't Corbitt have him walk up to the window, big as you please, and say, "Is there any mail here for Lee Corbitt?"

Or, was the box set up so men who didn't want to identify themselves could still get the mail that was addressed to them? That would account for the strange names. Now that he thought about it he remembered hearing that certain post offices on the western frontier had such mail put in a box and set out so the desperadoes and gunmen who roamed the territories could get their correspondence without giving their identities away.

If that were true it meant that Lee Corbitt was an outlaw and John had trouble believing that. More likely Corbitt was the kind of guy Waddy and his pa were in their younger days. He probably was forced to draw on someone who had a lot of friends and they were out to get him. He wasn't the sort to kill anyone else so he sort of hid out. That would account for his holing up in that miserable dugout instead of riding into town. It would also account for his sending John in to have the bay shod and do the other errands instead of making the trip himself.

The more John considered the matter the more certain he was that he had discovered the reason for his new companion's stealth. It made him think more than ever of Lee Corbitt. It showed that his friend was concerned about doing what was right.

John went to the post office, opened the packet of letters he had brought to mail and, without looking at them, gave them to the postmistress. Then he went out to the box and set to work, sorting through the letters. The problem was in trying to make out the names on the envelopes. Someone else had identified the letters as going to Gladstone, but the names were something else. They were written in pencil by fingers that were unused to forming words. Most of them almost defied deciphering. Finally, John located two pieces of mail that he was sure belonged to his friend. He stuffed them into his pocket and hurried to finish the errands Corbitt had sent him to do.

By the time he went back to the blacksmith's shop the shoeing was about finished. He only had a minute or so to wait for the broad-shouldered smithy to finish hammering the last nail into place. A short time later he picked up the saddlebags at McKenzie's and the supplies at the general store and was on his way back to the dugout. When he rode into the small yard, Corbitt came out to meet him.

"Got any mail?" he asked.

"A couple of letters." The boy dismounted, fished the mail from his pocket and shoved it into his companion's outstretched hand. He couldn't understand what there was to get so excited about, but by this time he had decided his companion was completely unpredictable.

While the older man read the mail, John unsaddled the sweating, dusty horse and rubbed him vigorously. The big bay was anxious to get to the water but John put a halter on him and tied him securely to a nearby tree. When the horse had cooled down he could drink his fill—not before.

The mail Corbitt got must have been good news. His spirits warmed measureably and he insisted on slicing several strips of bacon from the slab for their supper. John was curious about the change that had come over the older man so quickly, but waited for his companion to mention it.

"I got word from a couple of my old army pals," he said. "They're coming to see me! . . . And I just wrote to them today, asking what was keeping them. They probably won't get my letters, but I guess it don't matter. All I did was try to hurry them."

It seemed strange to John that two old friends would come out to the dugout to see Corbitt. From what the boy knew, his friend was a loner and not given to taking up with others. Anyone, that was, except him.

John knew Corbitt liked him. He showed it in a hundred ways. But that didn't change the fact that the man talked as though he didn't have anyone he was close to.

"When're they a-coming?" the boy asked.

Corbitt toyed with the last of his bacon. "I expect them most any time. . . . " With that he stood and went over to the saddlebags, taking something from one of them. "What d'you think of this?" he asked, laying a new Smith and Wesson .32 on the table in front of him.

John stared. He recognized it as the best gun McKenzie carried.

"You didn't get this for *me?*" he asked, his voice void of emotion.

Corbitt allowed a thin smile to crack the solemnity of his features. "I use a Colt," he said.

Carefully John picked it up. It was light in weight and nicely balanced—one of the finest guns he had ever seen.

"What d'you think of it?" Corbitt asked.

"I . . . I can't take it."

"Why not? It's yours. I bought it for you."

"I know, but like I said. I can't be beholden to you any more than I am now. And I ain't got the money to pay for it." Reluctantly he laid the gun back on the table. "So, I can't take it."

"I thought we settled that. You're a-going to work for me."

John's eyes narrowed. "Doing what?"

Corbitt laughed. "Don't worry about it. I'll tell you when the time comes."

The following morning John strapped on the new six-gun and went out to try it. It came up quickly, smoothly and he was able to squeeze the trigger with a new assurance that he would hit his target. He didn't realize Corbitt had joined him until he emptied the cylinder and was reloading.

"How does it feel?" Corbitt asked quietly.

"Better'n any gun I ever used."

The older man nodded. "That was all you needed. Not that the Colt ain't a good weapon. It's one of the best. It's just too heavy for you till you've growed some."

After half an hour of practice John saddled

Rusty and rode him along the river for something to do. He didn't know about Corbitt, but he, for one, was getting anxious to move. Waiting around as they had been since they made camp in the old dugout had been tiresome—a lot worse than if they had been working hard. If he was going to be on Corbitt's payroll, he wanted to get at it so he could start paying for that new gun. If he wasn't, he wanted to get on the road so he could find work somewhere.

He was still thinking about the matter when he rode back into the yard several hours later. Even before reaching the dugout he saw there were three strange horses in the old corral. The animals were a cut above the average cowhand's mount. They were heavier, with powerful chests and well-developed leg muscles; horses like the bay Corbitt rode—and like his own Rusty, John noted with considerable satisfaction. No sirree, he didn't have to be ashamed of having his horse stand alongside the others.

Corbitt's friends had finally arrived. Only there were three, instead of two. Young Breckenridge unsaddled his mount, curried him briskly, and, after he cooled down, took him to the river to drink. Then he tethered him in an area where the grass was tall and lush.

It was midafternoon when he walked back to the dugout, approaching it from the side where there were no windows. The wind had ceased and a stifling, breathless hush had settled over the riverbank, save for the restless movement of the horses as the flies tormented them. The door to the crude building was open and, though the men inside were talking softly, John was able to hear at least part of what they were saying.

". . . Now, who's coming with the extra horses?" Corbitt asked.

"Little Ike Haynes and Obed Metzner," one of the strangers said. "They'll be riding in some time after dark."

"Everybody know exactly what he's supposed to do?" Corbitt asked.

John shifted nervously from one foot to the other. He felt uncomfortable standing there at the corner of the sod wall listening, but he couldn't force himself to leave.

"Now, I'm going to ask you one more time. You all know what you're to do tomorrow?" Corbitt repeated, his voice rising. "We can't have no slipups."

He waited as each man assured him in turn that he knew his assignment. John felt the sweat pearl on his forehead and he wiped it away with a shaking hand. He didn't know what was going on but he didn't like the sound of it. Whatever they were about had to be against the law. And Lee Corbitt wasn't just one of the men. He was the leader.

"What I'm wondering about," one of the newcomers blurted loudly, "is that kid. Are we going to be able to trust him?"

"Yep."

"You're sure of that?"

"I said don't worry about him! He don't know nothing but he'll come around. And he's going to be a big help. He's working out with a gun now and he's a-going to be lightning fast! Give him another six months or so and there won't be none of us, including me, who'd dare to face him!"

John Breckenridge felt the strength seep from his legs and his breathing grow shallow and rapid.

His stomach twisted in an agonizing knot. He still didn't know what was going to take place, but for the first time he realized that his friend Corbitt wasn't what he thought he was. He was riding the outlaw trail!

He was motionless when the horses in the corral suddenly became alert. Their heads came up quickly. Ears twitched and one of them nickered.

Someone was coming! John dived for the brush—and just in time. A moment later two men rode in leading a remuda of six fresh horses.

7

John sprawled in the willows, pressing tensely against the parched ground, scarcely daring to breathe. His heart hammered so savagely against his ribs he was sure it would give him away. The men sauntered out of the dugout to meet the two newcomers.

"I thought you wasn't to be here till after dark!" Corbitt snapped.

The younger of the two strangers rested his long, thin fingers on the saddle horn and leaned forward. A mocking grin creased his smooth face. "Ain't ya even going to say howdy?"

The leader's eyes narrowed and his voice was harsh and strained. "Not till I find out how come you're here in broad daylight. . . . Anybody see you?"

"Now what kind of a question is that?" Little Ike demanded. "We know what we're doing, me and Obed. Of course nobody seen us!"

Lee turned to the older man. "How about it, Obed? Think you was seen?"

The gray-haired man with the wide, bristling moustache and sunken eyes shook his head. "Ain't no way anybody could have. We picked up the remuda and came across country all the way. Didn't even get seen by no jackrabbit. You don't have to worry, boss. We're plumb clean."

Finally satisfied, Corbitt motioned carelessly toward the corral. "Put the horses in there and come to the house. We want to go over things so you'll both know what's a-going on."

One of the rough-looking gang who had been inside with Corbitt, went to the corner of the dugout and looked across the river.

"Come on, Fey," Lee ordered. "We got things to do before the kid comes back."

"That's exactly what I'm wondering about," Allen Fey said. "Where is that kid, anyhow?"

John trembled violently and for a moment feared that the beady-eyed Fey saw him where he was lying. He resisted a sudden urge to jump to his feet and bolt in a desperate attempt to reach Rusty and get away.

"He went off on his horse an hour or so before you got here," Corbitt said. "He does that all the time."

The gunman drew in a deep breath. "What's he riding? A sorrel?"

"Yeah. What about it?"

"There's a big sorrel grazing down there by the river, and there ain't no sign of the kid anywhere."

Corbitt laughed. "If that sorrel's there, you can bet he ain't far away. You never seen anyone take better care of a horse than he does."

Fey still was not satisfied. "I don't like it, Lee. You oughta know by this time you can't trust kids. They'll sneak around on cat's feet when you least expect 'em. And they'll hear things you sure don't want 'em to."

"That ain't nothin' to worry about. He don't suspect nothin'. But if he ain't here by the time we get done talking, we'll go find him."

82

"It can't happen too soon to suit me," Fey mumbled, turning back to the ramshackle shelter.

John lay motionless until Obed and Little Ike had the horses in the corral and joined the others in the dugout. His first thought was to get down to Rusty, saddle and bridle him and ride across the river and as far away from that gang of men as he could. He wouldn't have his bedroll or any grub or his pa's rifle and Colt Peacemaker. He wouldn't even have much ammunition for the Smith and Wesson. He *had* to stay till he could figure a way to get his gear. And with so many around he didn't know how he could manage that.

John didn't see how he could go back to the house and sit there listening to them guys talk when he knew they were planning something crooked. But he had to! He didn't have any choice. And he had to get out of where he was, pronto, before that Allen Fey—whoever he was—talked Lee into sending someone out to look for him. If he was caught that close, they'd *know* he had heard them and he'd be in bad trouble!

Turning quickly he crawled down the slope toward Rusty. He had just reached his horse and stood up by the big sorrel when Corbitt came to the corner of the building and called for him.

"I'm down here with Rusty!" he shouted, hoping his voice didn't betray his concern.

"Come up when you've finished!"

For several minutes he worked with his mount, rubbing Rusty's withers and going over his back. Then young Breckenridge turned and headed slowly for the dugout.

Corbitt came to the door to meet him. There was no warmth or friendliness in his lean, hard face. "Where you been, kid?" he demanded, harshly.

83

"For a ride along the river," he said. "Like I told you. I had to give Rusty some exercise. I ain't ridden him for almost a week." He glanced into the dugout. "I see your friends is here."

The leader ignored his remark. "When'd you get back, kid?"

"A little while ago." He knew he ought to be looking Corbitt directly in the eyes, but he couldn't. He was too uneasy about lying.

"How long ago?"

"Long enough to get Rusty staked out and taken care of."

That seemed to satisfy his friend.

"Rustle up some buffalo chips and wood. Obed's promised to fix us some of his salt pork and beans. He was a cook in our old Tennessee regiment."

Pleased to have passed the test, young Breckenridge scurried to do as he was told. He went up on the prairie and soon had a double armload of buffalo chips. There was something about the tone of Corbitt's voice that was disturbing, but John couldn't place the reason for it. He went back to the dugout, loudly humming snatches of a ballad so they would know he was approaching. He didn't want to make Fey or anyone else think he had overheard them.

He was going to start the fire the way he always had, but Obed already had it going and the beans were boiling in the kettle. It was then he realized what upset him. He had seen smoke pouring out of the makeshift chimney as he and Corbitt were talking. That indicated Obed was already hard at work, fixing supper. Corbitt must have sent him for fuel to get him out of the way so they could finish talking.

And that was all right with John. He realized the danger of his situation. These were desperate men who used their guns first and talked afterwards. There probably wasn't one of them who would hesitate to shoot him if they thought he was a risk. He had to be very careful if he wanted to get out of here alive. His hand crept back to the bone handle of the Smith and Wesson. For the first time he was thankful for the lighter caliber gun. He probably couldn't stand up to any of the gang when it came to the draw; men like that were quick to shoot. But there was one thing he knew: he wasn't going down without a fight.

He deposited the chips in a box beside the stove and went back for a load of wood when they called him to supper. The sun was on the horizon and the long shadows were growing. Inside the dugout the gloom of the approaching night spread from the doorway to the far reaches of the room. Obed had set a candle on the warming oven so he could see to work, but the men sat in virtual darkness.

There was excitement in the air and everyone laughed and talked a lot—a little too much, it seemed to John. It was as though they were trying to force from their minds the dread of what they were planning. Then he noticed the row of bottles on the table and realized they were doing more drinking than eating. He put some beans and salt pork on his plate and Obed set a cup of coffee before him.

"Here," Fey said, reaching for the bottle. "Better sweeten up that coffee." He would have poured a generous charge of whiskey into John's cup but the boy put a hand over it.

"I don't want that stuff."

"What's wrong with it?" the older man snarled, his tongue stumbling over the words. "Think you're too good to drink with us?"

John felt the color rise in his cheeks. "I don't want it."

Fey was about to insist again, even more forcefully, but Corbitt stopped him. "That's enough!" he rasped.

However, the other man was too drunk to be stopped. "When I ask a body to drink with me I expect him to drink. If he don't I figger it's because he thinks he's too good for me!"

"Nobody's drinking any more tonight," the leader said, jerking the bottle from the drunken gunman's hands. "Elim, you and Little Ike get them other bottles and put them away. You can drink yourself stupid all you want to after tomorrow, but not till then."

Fey pushed himself away from the table and staggered to his feet. "Nobody's a-going to tell *me* when I can drink and when I can't."

Corbitt stepped close to him. "Sit," he snarled.

"Who says so?"

"Fey, I ain't telling you again!"

He did as he was told, grumbling darkly.

"Elim," Corbitt called to his right-hand man, "take that whiskey outside and pour it on the ground."

Two or three groaned their disapproval.

"Don't pour it *all* out," one of the gang protested. "We'll need a drink or two in the morning."

"Save one bottle. But give it to me. I'll keep it till tomorrow." Corbitt faced Allen Fey. "Any objections?"

The gunman continued to mutter but it was obvious he was not going to challenge Corbitt.

The confrontation between the two men dampened the excitement and liquor-reinforced gaiety of the occasion. The men fell silent and one by one they got up from the table and made their way outside. There they rolled cigarettes and smoked.

Corbitt circulated among them until he was certain the lid was tightly on and there would be no more trouble. Then he went back inside where John, who was still sitting at the table, stared into the darkness.

"It's going to be too hot to sleep in here," Corbitt said. "Get your bedroll and we'll go down by the river."

The boy did as he was told, picking up his rifle and his pa's six-gun. With Corbitt there he probably wouldn't have a chance to sneak away, but he wanted those guns, just in case.

"What're you taking them for?" the leader demanded.

"I . . . I thought we might need them."

"Put them back."

"B-B-But. . . ."

"I said, *put them back!*" John did as he was told. They went some distance from the others and put down their bedrolls.

"If you do as I say," Corbitt began abruptly, "we won't have no trouble. You and me will travel together. We'll make a good team."

"Is . . . is *this* the kind of work you figgered I'd be doing?" John blurted.

Corbitt's eyes narrowed in the semi-darkness and John could see the muscles about his lips begin to twitch. "What do you mean, '*this* kind of work'?"

"You know what I mean," John continued

recklessly. "You didn't get that gang together just to talk. You're figgering on robbing the stage or a bank or something like that!"

Corbitt looked quickly away, drawing in four or five deep breaths. At last he turned back to his companion. "I didn't plan on letting you know nothing about it till tomorrow when we got back," he said. "But I guess it don't make no difference. You ain't going to have no chance to get away."

John thought Corbitt would go on, explaining what they were planning, but he did not. He unrolled his bedroll, fashioned a cigarette, and lit it with a sulfur match. For a long while after he finished and had ground it into the dirt with his heel, he sat there, looking off into space. Young Breckenridge spread out his own bedroll and crawled into it.

Finally Corbitt came and stood over him. "Don't spoil everything by trying to run out on me," he said in a harsh whisper. "Understand?"

The boy nodded wordlessly.

"It won't do you no good to take off. Before you got two miles me and the boys'd have you in our sights. There ain't one of them wouldn't shoot you if it came to that."

The boy swallowed hard.

"Even old Obed would shoot quick as that, should you try to run out on him. In case you don't know it, he'll be watching you tomorrow while we're gone." He was breathing heavily. "Don't let his gray hair fool you. . . . I've seen him use that iron of his cool as ice in January. And not all that long ago, neither. Last summer out in Wyoming Territory was the last I know about."

John Breckenridge lay on his back in the bedroll, staring up at the cloudless, star-dotted sky. He hadn't felt so torn apart and miserable since Ma died and he learned Waddy didn't want him around any more. His young chest ached and his stomach twisted into a tight knot; nausea swept over him. His emotions were a confused jumble. Lee Corbitt wasn't just anybody; he had saved John's life. Still, John could not ignore his friend's actions of the past few hours. His conscience shouted that something was wrong—that Corbitt was not what John had first thought him to be.

John knew what Waddy would say: Believe the best about a friend and stand up for him until you find out for sure he is wrong. But when that happens, be just as quick to accept the truth and act accordingly. "That's what we've got minds for," his stepfather had said so often. "We're supposed to use them."

Young Breckenridge closed his eyes and tried to sleep, but his tortured mind churned wildly. Once or twice he raised on one elbow and looked over at his companion. The instant he moved Corbitt was awake and sitting up.

"Lay down and go to sleep," the older man ordered sternly.

"I can't."

"You've got to! We'll have a long, hard ride tomorrow."

"Are . . . are we going to leave them other guys?" John asked, hopefully. "Is it going to be just you and me?"

"Maybe. We'll have to see."

At that he relaxed slightly, telling himself that Corbitt didn't intend to stay on the outlaw trail. He tried to make himself believe that was the way it was, but in his heart he knew differently. Everything he had heard since the rough, hard-bitten strangers arrived had underscored the fact that Corbitt was their leader, he had called the men together and was planning the robbery. As hard as John tried to find excuses for his friend he always came back to the same cold, hard fact: Corbitt was an outlaw.

The boy twisted and turned sleeplessly, wishing the night to end, but dreading the coming day. Toward morning he dozed, but when he awakened, shortly before sunup, the gnawing ache returned to knife into his stomach.

Apparently Corbitt wasn't sleeping well either. As long as John remained motionless, his companion lay quite still. The instant he stirred, however, Corbitt sat up, glancing quickly at the boy. Morning finally came, and the outlaw's lips parted as if to say something, but he clamped his teeth on the unspoken words, threw his blanket aside, and pulled on his boots.

Silently the two went back to the dugout. Although it was still so early that the first rays of the sun were only narrow gray streaks on the distant eastern horizon, the men were up and had their horses saddled. Obed was frying pancakes and boiling coffee on the battered old stove.

"Coming in for breakfast, John?" Corbitt asked at the door.

"I don't feel like eating."

"Better have something, anyway. Might be quite a spell before you get anything as good as Obed's flapjacks again." The words were spoken mildly, but John caught the steel in them, the veiled order to do as he was told. Mechanically he followed Corbitt into the semi-dark building and sat down beside him.

The others were already at the table. Some

had finished breakfast; others were still eating. John and Corbitt ate in comparative silence. When the older man had completed his meal he rolled and smoked a cigarette, then turned to the older of the Haynes brothers. "Time to go, Elim," he said quietly.

The rawboned gunman across the table got to his feet and spoke to the others. Obediently they filed outside, leaving Corbitt and John alone at the table. When the door closed, the leader turned and spoke again, almost in the boy's ear. His voice was soft. "You're a-going to be alone with Obed, but remember what I told you about not trying anything. His orders are to keep you here one way or another. And there's one thing about old Obed: he does what he's told."

John moistened his lips with his tongue and nodded helplessly.

"Another thing. When he tells you what to do, you do it! Got that?"

Before young Breckenridge could answer, Elim was back. "We're ready when you are."

"Fine." Corbitt glanced at John as though there was something else he wanted to say, but instead, he turned abruptly and strode outside.

8

John went to the door in time to see his friend mount a stalwart black steed and ride off at the head of the desperate band. He couldn't understand why Corbitt didn't use his own horse. The black was a good animal—John had noticed this when Obed and Ike Haynes brought the remuda in—but the bay could run him into the ground. John supposed Corbitt had a good reason for not riding his own horse, but he didn't know what it could be. He was still standing there when Obed came up beside him, his gaunt frame all but filling the doorway.

"Where're they a-going?" John asked. His voice was numb and expressionless. "And what're they a-going to do?"

The gray-haired cook and wrangler hesitated. "Guess it won't hurt none to tell you. You'll find out soon enough. . . . They're heading for Gladstone. They're fixing to knock off the bank."

Young Breckenridge gasped.

"Don't let yourself get so shook up. Corbitt knows what he's doing. He'll come back without a scratch and the part still in his hair. He's a cool one, that feller. Ain't nobody in these parts as can get the best of him."

John swallowed against the lump in his throat. "I wasn't thinking about him!" he blurted.

Obed laid a hand on the boy's shoulder. "To tell you the truth, I didn't reckon you was."

"How long till they get back?" he asked.

Obed spit a wad of tobacco juice in the direction of a grasshopper, missing him by a scant half inch. "I reckon they ought to be back here by noon, iffen everything goes right. It won't take long to walk into that bank, scoop up the money, and get outta there."

John wiped the sweat from his forehead. Then, deliberately, he turned and glanced at Rusty. "Think I'll go down and take care of my horse."

The old man nodded. "You do that. Only don't forget: The last thing Corbitt told me was to see that you don't run off. . . . I like you, kid. I sure enough wouldn't want to have to hurt you. So, you do as I say."

The boy's cheeks colored guiltily. "I ain't going no place."

"Or try to take off?" the old man persisted.

"What kind of a guy do you think I am, anyway?"

"One with a powerful sight of backbone!" Obed said in admiration. "Enough to cause you to try most anything, if ya felt strong enough about it."

John's eyes flashed. "You've leveled with me. I'm a-going to level with you." He swallowed hard. "I may not get away till they get back, but I'm a-going! I don't care what Corbitt or anybody says. Ma and my step-pa didn't bring me up to be no bank robber!"

To the boy's surprise Obed's hard eyes softened. "Wisht I'd had the courage you got, John, back when I was your age and had to decide which way I was a-going. 'Deed I do. My life'd be a sight different now." His features grew stern. "But that don't mean I won't do what I have to to keep you here. Remember that!"

Young Breckenridge went down to his horse, loosed the rope that tethered him, and took him to the river for water. If he had had his guns, his bedroll, and some grub, he'd have taken off. Obed's threats wouldn't have stopped him. He knew the old man was good enough with a rifle to put the fear into anyone he was shooting at, but John also knew that he could have Rusty into the brush and out of sight before his companion was even aware of what was going on. And, after Obed found out what John was doing, it would take awhile to start after him. The old man would have to hobble out to the corral, catch up a horse, and saddle and bridle him. By that time John and Rusty would be a mile or two down the trail. And with a horse as fast as Rusty, that was more time than he would need.

But, of course, the boy could not think about shucking out. His guns and gear were in the dugout and his saddle and bridle were outside where the old man would be sure to see what he was doing if he tried to get them. No, he couldn't get away now; he would have to wait.

He was still currying Rusty when Obed came to the corner of the old dugout and called to him. "Better get them other horses watered, boy. The boys're apt to be back before we know it. And when they get here, they're a-going to be bent on cutting west for parts beyond. They won't like it none if we ain't got them horses ready to go."

Reluctantly, John carried out his orders. He had to help Obed because he was afraid not to. The old man talked about his courage, but John didn't feel very brave right then. When he finished watering the remuda, Obed sent him up on the bluff to watch for the men.

"And when ya see them coming, sing out proper-like and scoot back down here to help me. They're a-going to be in an all-fired hurry to change horses and get a-going!"

Young Breckenridge climbed to the top of the bluff and, shielding his eyes with the broad brim of his sweat-stained hat he stared across the scorching prairie in the direction of Gladstone. He didn't have long to wait; in a few minutes he saw the faint plume of dust in the distance. The thin gray puffs seemed to rise a few feet higher than the riders' heads and hang there as though suspended by some invisible support before falling back to the parched ground.

"They're a-coming!" he shouted.

The old man was outside the door in an instant. "Are they close enough to tell how many they are?"

At first John wasn't able to separate the riders from each other, but as he watched he was able to make them out. "There're only three!"

"Are ya sure?"

"Positive! And they're a-riding like old Satan himself is after them!"

"There's been trouble," Obed exclaimed. "Get down here, boy! We've got work to do."

They set into the task feverishly. They had just finished haltering the best horses in the remuda, including Corbitt's big bay, when the riders pounded in and slid to a stop in a small cloud of dust that billowed up around their horses' feet.

"Get them horses saddled!" Corbitt snapped as he slid from the back of his trembling steed and headed for the dugout. "We've got a little business to tend to. Then we gotta get out of here, pronto."

"Where's Fey and that side kick of his?" Obed asked.

"That dumb-headed Fey got trigger happy and shot the clerk," the leader said. "And the whole town exploded. Them two never got farther'n the back door on their way out. They was both cut down."

"Come on!" Elim called from inside the crude structure. "We've got to get that money divided and get outta here. There's no telling when that posse'll be on our trail."

But Corbitt did not join him immediately. "Obed," he said, keeping his voice down, "get the kid's sorrel saddled. He's a-riding with me."

The old man's features were inscrutable. "I figgered ya wouldn't dare leave him behind."

While the three who had actually robbed the bank counted the money and divided it, Obed and John saddled and bridled fresh mounts for them. Young Breckenridge was quivering as he worked. He was helping the bank robbers to get away. Did that mean he was guilty, too?

"Better get your gear," Obed said when the last horse was saddled. "I'll get that Rusty horse of yours."

"I don't need no horse," John retorted, defiantly. "I ain't going nowhere."

Obed's bony fingers tightened convulsively on the thin shoulder blade of the boy beside him. "Listen, kid. Corbitt's riled already. If ya know what's good for ya, you'll do as you're told."

Something in the gray-haired man's voice made John see that he was speaking the truth.

When the leader came out of the dugout minutes later, John was already astride Rusty.

"We've got to split up," Corbitt ordered crisply. "I'll take the kid. You three go together. We'll meet in Dobytown or Lowell, Nebraska, soon as things quiet down. If we get there first, we'll wait for you. If you make it before we do, wait for us."

With a wave of his hand, Elim led his brother and Obed away in a south-easterly direction. Corbitt swung into the saddle without speaking to his young companion and galloped away, expecting John to follow. They crossed the river upstream from the dugout and took to the hills, angling in the opposite direction the others had taken.

John rode in silence. The way he saw it, he wasn't going to get away from Corbitt, at least for a time. Obed was right; the outlaw was keeping a close watch on every move he made. A certain queasiness gripped him and there was a numbing pain in his stomach—a nagging ache that refused to go away.

Corbitt kept moving at a punishing pace and the boy had no choice but to keep up, as difficult as it was for him to push the big sorrel so hard. Once or twice Corbitt slowed to a walk until the mounts had caught their breath before again maintaining the blistering pace they had started with.

"We can't keep riding so hard," John protested. "We're a-going to wind our horses and maybe kill them."

Corbitt glared at him and his words rasped harshly. "Unless you're a-hankering to go to jail and risk getting your neck stretched, we've got to keep going!"

"Me?" the boy echoed defensively. "I ain't done nothing!"

"You're a-riding with me. That makes you as guilty as I am."

John fell silent once more. He could argue with Corbitt about making him ride along, but that wouldn't do any good. The outlaw leader had decided they would ride together and there was nothing he could do to change that.

Breckenridge looked over his shoulder continually, expecting to see the dust of the posse rising behind them. The posse was on their trail; he was sure of that. And, sooner or later, they would catch up. He steeled himself against it, trying not to think about what it would be like to be hauled back to Gladstone and thrown in jail. He hadn't done anything he was ashamed of. But he supposed Corbitt was right: nobody would believe him.

Hour after hour they rode. John couldn't believe they had been able to throw the posse off the trail so completely, but there was no sign they were being followed. He and Corbitt continued to push their mounts over the rough ground as savagely as they could without winding their horses. It was late in the afternoon and the sun was slipping rapidly toward the western horizon, throwing long shadows across the drought-browned prairie. On a slight rise, Corbitt reined in and stood in the stirrups to stare at the dark shapes near the river a couple of miles ahead.

"The buffalo. Just as I figgered," he murmured. "Now, we'll throw that posse off so far they'll *never* be able to find us!"

Young Breckenridge wondered what he was planning, but the outlaw didn't wait for questions. He raked the bay's flanks with his spurs, and the powerful animal responded immediately, bursting into a long, effortless gallop. John did the same.

Corbitt saw that the vast herd was moving slowly westward, grazing as they went. He veered in that direction, riding at an angle that would intersect the route the big herd was taking, a mile or two ahead of the lead bulls. Toward the north side of the area that soon would be crossed by the buffalo, the outlaw stopped, stepped off his horse and jerked an old blanket from one of his saddle-bags. Tearing it into eight pieces he threw four of them to John.

"Wrap Rusty's feet the way I'm doing," he ordered. "And be quick about it!"

John had heard Waddy tell about that trick to blot out the hoofprints of a horse. The cloth wouldn't last long, but it could provide time, even if the tracker were experienced.

Moments later they rode on swiftly, for the herd had spotted them and the lead animals were getting restive. If the animals turned, Corbitt's little surprise for the posse would be spoiled. He did not relax until they were well out of the big herd's path.

"Now what do we do?" the boy asked.

"We'll ride to the river—it ain't more than a mile over there—and go into the water. Our trail will disappear back where the buffalo tramp it out." He laughed drily. "They'll think we grabbed onto the feet of a hawk and flew away!"

They rode until they reached the brush and trees along the Platte. Then they entered the water and headed east, allowing their horses to walk slowly in the center of the stream.

"I think we're far enough," Corbitt said when they had traveled more than three miles. "We'll find a campsite and hole up. Our horses need rest and so do we."

John dismounted quickly and loosed the cinch. He would have removed the saddle but his companion stopped him.

"Don't do that. We might have to get out of here in a hurry."

John did as he was directed. He curried the big sorrel and located a spot to tether him where the grass was heavy and green. When he got back to the place where his companion had spread out his bedroll, Corbitt had something for them to eat.

"We'll have to be satisfied with jerky and cold water tonight," he said. "We can't risk having anyone see our smoke."

When they finished eating, John was about to spread out his own bedroll some distance from Corbitt's and turn in. It had been a long, trying day and he was exhausted. But the outlaw called him over.

"I've got something for you." He handed the boy a fistful of bills.

"What's this?" John demanded.

"Your share of our little caper this morning."

Young Breckenridge had never seen so much money at one time in his entire life, but he made no move to take it. "I didn't have nothing to do with robbing that bank."

"You had as big a part as Obed and he got a share."

"But. . . ."

"If you're a-worrying about paying for that gun I bought you, you can pay me outta your share. I wrote down what it cost."

Still John remained motionless. "It ain't mine."

Corbitt's face hardened. "I don't want to have to argue with ya. Take them bills and put them in your pocket." Reluctantly, the boy did as he was told.

"We'd better turn in," the outlaw said, starting for his blankets. "We've got a lot of hard riding the next few days."

The money weighed heavily in John's pocket. It was the first time he had knowingly had anything in his possession that was stolen. It made him feel unclean inside—dirtiness that soap and water couldn't wash away. He lay with his eyes closed, but he could not even try to go to sleep. He wasn't going to spend any of the money, of that he was sure. Yet, if the posse caught up with them, that money would be another damning piece of evidence. Who would believe that he wasn't going to use it? And how could he get Corbitt to take it back?

Darkness settled over the riverbank and John's weariness increased. Still, he did not even try to sleep. He didn't hear his companion snoring and wondered if Corbitt was also lying awake. After a time the outlaw crawled out of his bedroll and pulled on his boots. "I'm a-going to have a look around."

Young Breckenridge watched him pick up his rifle and move off into the night. For several minutes the boy lay tensely, listening to his companion's footsteps heading up the hill away from the river. *This is it!* he thought to himself suddenly, *the chance I've been waiting for to get away!*

Hurriedly, John crawled out of his blankets, rolled them, and picked up his rifle. As quietly as possible he stole toward the place where Rusty was grazing. He put the bridle on his big sorrel and tightened the cinch. His heart was hammering fiercely as he climbed into the saddle and urged the horse into the water.

For a moment fear tortured him as he heard the splashing of Rusty's big hooves. He was certain Corbitt would hear and come after him, but there was no sound of the outlaw following. The boy urged Rusty out of the water onto the north bank and up the steep slope.

After Corbitt had satisfied himself that no one was nearby, he returned to camp. The instant he stepped out of the willows he realized that something was wrong. The big sorrel was not to be seen and John's bedroll was gone. That kid! That stubborn, hard-headed kid had taken off! He should've known better than to give him that money.

On the way to his horse, Corbitt dashed past the place where the boy had bedded down. He went by the spot and turned back, curiously. The new revolver and holster were on top and the money was beneath them, a slim stack of bills. Without even counting, he knew they were all there. He paused long enough to pick them up.

The outlaw mounted his big bay, but for a moment remained stock still. It was too dark to follow John's trail. Which direction had he gone? How far ahead was he?

That horse of John's was faster than most and strong enough to keep going when even his own bay was wind-broken. What good would it do to try to follow the kid in the dark? He would have to wait until daylight and by then John would be so far ahead there would be no catching him.

Corbitt cursed the day he had saved the boy's hide, but he was a practical man. Since he couldn't catch John, it was best to hit the trail, putting as much distance between himself and this campsite as possible in case the kid led the authorities here.

Hurriedly he packed his own gear and moved out. Their trails would cross again, his and the kid's. And when that happened there'd be one sorry boy! *Nobody* pulled out on Lee Corbitt and got away with it.

9

John Breckenridge leaned forward in the saddle until his head was close to the big sorrel's shaggy mane as he coaxed more speed from the valiant horse. Rusty burst out of the cottonwoods along the river and raced over the rough ground toward the trail. The entire area was pocked with gopher holes and prairie dog towns. John prayed that Rusty would miss them. If his horse caught a hoof in a hole at that speed it would be the end of the big gelding and his rider.

Grimly, the boy forced such thoughts from his mind. He dare not pull the horse in, at least not till they were far enough away from Corbitt to be safe. He threatened to be an even greater menace than gopher or prairie dog holes. Corbitt had warned John not to run away, so the outlaw would surely be on the boy's trail.

It hurt John to push his mount so hard. Rusty had been moving fast all day and was quite weary. When they had stopped on the other side of the river a few hours earlier, the sorrel's powerful legs and chest were quivering with fatigue. For a time the gelding had stood motionless, too weary even to graze.

Now his young master was calling upon him again and he responded, more from will than strength. He was the sort of horse that would run till he dropped, if called upon to do so. John knew this and it tore at him, yet he had no choice; he had to demand more of Rusty than ever before.

Everything depended upon Rusty and the stamina and speed still left in those sturdy legs and courageous heart. The sorrel was going to have to outrun and outlast Corbitt's bay. Although he had a few minute's start, he knew that keeping ahead of the outlaw would be a large order: one he didn't know whether he was capable of or not.

John relaxed slightly as he reached the trail that paralleled the river, and he turned east on it. The danger from his pursuer was still as great as ever, but at least he didn't have to be so concerned about Rusty stepping into a hole and breaking a leg.

The tall horse seemed to sense the urgency of the moment. He was flying along the deeply rutted trail with all the strength he could summon. John could feel his mount's labored breathing with his knees, and his hand on Rusty's neck was wet with the animal's sweat. But, obediently, the great-hearted sorrel was running as he had never run before.

A few more minutes and young Breckenridge noted a subtle change in the rhythmic flow of Rusty's legs and his labored breathing. It was a change John had never been aware of in all the riding he had done. Instinctively he recognized it as ominous: Rusty was at the very limit of his endurance.

The boy straightened and put a slight pressure on the reins. At that moment he didn't care whether Corbitt caught up with him or not. He wasn't going to continue punishing his horse. The sorrel came to a stop and stood, spraddle-legged. His head was down and his nostrils flared as his chest heaved with each tortured breath. John dismounted and loosed the cinch. Desperately he willed Rusty to keep standing.

"That's all right, boy," he murmured softly. "Just take it easy. We ain't going no farther."

After a time the big sorrel began to breathe easier and the trembling left his powerful legs. Young Breckenridge picked up the reins and slowly led his mount over to the trees. When he was certain Rusty had cooled down he took him to the river to drink and tied him in the grass along the bank. Only then did John crawl into his bedroll and close his eyes. He wasn't going to sleep, he told himself. He would only rest awhile, waiting for Corbitt to catch up with him. That was inevitable. When his former friend decided he was going to do something, he did it.

Young Breckenridge was so exhausted, however, that he soon drifted into a deep sleep. Once or twice the anguish of the day troubled him so much he stirred restlessly and sat up, trying to figure out where he was and why the pain in his stomach was so fierce and persistent; the gnawing pangs of hunger gripped him. He had seen that Rusty was fed, but had been so concerned about Corbitt being on his trail that he hadn't eaten himself. He decided he would get up soon and take a little jerky from his saddlebags. But he was so exhausted he went back to sleep before he could do so.

The following morning as the sun came up, his hunger nagged him awake. He slipped out of his blankets and built a little fire to fix breakfast.

It would be the only meal he would eat until supper, a practice he had picked up from Corbitt, who didn't want to take the time for a noon meal when he was traveling.

John could not understand why the outlaw hadn't found him. The idea that Corbitt hadn't followed was unthinkable. That meant his pursuer was somewhere behind, pressing hard to close the gap.

It was early morning and the coolest portion of the day was at hand. Cautiously John went out to where the stout sorrel was grazing. Rusty's head came up swiftly as the young rider approached and his nostrils widened.

"Easy, boy," John murmured. He looked the gelding over, watching for signs of soreness or stiff muscles that would make him lame. But if there were any, John could not detect them.

Satisfied that his horse was again able to travel, he went back to the campsite, repacked his bedroll, and saddled up. Taking advantage of the fact that the August sun was still low on the horizon and wasn't yet blasting the almost treeless prairie with its flaming rays, he rode briskly back to the trail. Dew was still on the yucca and milkweed, and the scalding wind slept.

That morning John kept an eye on his horse as he rode. He had to be sure Rusty had fully recovered from the harrowing trail of the day before. After being on the move for some time, he stopped and, walking backwards, led the sorrel for a hundred yards or so in order to be positive there were no visible signs of lameness after the long, hard ride. As far as he could determine, however, there were none. Rusty held his head high and his gait was swift and spirited, evidence of the fact that the boy had him in excellent condition.

John remounted and allowed the gelding to step out quickly until the sun climbed higher in the pale, azure sky and aimed its fiery darts at every living thing that moved on the bleak, seared plains. Then he took Rusty down to the shade of the cottonwoods and allowed him to rest.

Despite the concern for his horse, the boy kept a wary eye on the trail behind him for signs of his former friend. Twice he veered into the hills to the left and doubled back to take a closer look at the stretch he had just covered. He studied the area intently, his keen young eyes searching the broad valley and the thin swath of trees that hid the Platte from view, yet there was no evidence that he was being followed.

It was almost night when he stopped again, this time to rest till morning. He still had seen no evidence that the horse was showing any ill effects from the stress of the day before, but he was not going to take a chance on hurting him.

A few miles west of the settlement of North Platte, well into Nebraska Territory, he forded the shallow river and headed across country to the Republican. Once on the other side of the narrow, muddy stream he struck out over the Kansas hills, angling eastward for Abilene.

Several days later he reached the robust, noisy settlement. It was late in the afternoon when he rode into the brawling community that was just beginning to come into its own as a cow town. He entered the Kansas town from the north, riding by a number of homes before turning east to go past the feed store, the Wells Fargo Express Office, and the blacksmith shop on his way to the livery stable. The farmers and ranchers who had come into town for supplies were on their way home and the saloon customers hadn't yet ridden in. Young Breckenridge noted a wagon and two saddled horses were tethered to the hitching rail in front of the land office. At the far end of the street, small boys were rolling hoops in front of a ramshackle house.

John's funds were dangerously low, but he took Rusty to the livery barn where he insisted on currying and feeding him himself. Once that was done, he crossed the street to the barbershop where he treated himself to a bath and a haircut. He had to get cleaned up, even though that meant dipping even further into his paltry supply of money, but he also had another reason for visiting the barber: there was no better place in town to get information. Bartenders, waiters, and hotel clerks were usually as close-mouthed as the local marshal. But not the barber. As Waddy Ross used to say, a barber's tongue was loose at both ends. With that in mind John took a bath, which cost him a quarter, and seated himself in the chair for a haircut. In a few moments they were talking about the herds traveling up from Texas.

"What's a nice kid like you want to know about them Johnny Rebs?" the barber asked, contempt in his voice.

"I was figgering on hitting them for a job."

The barber stopped working, his comb and scissors poised above the boy's head. "There ain't much other work around here, that's a fact."

"Seen any of them trail bosses still around?"

"They don't come up in the respectable part of town much," the barber said. "Mostly they're south of the tracks in them saloons and sporting places along Texas Street. They associate with the greasers and riffraff. Decent folks won't pay them no mind." He set to work again. "But my guess is that most of them has headed back south. They're up here with their herds by early summer to ship east. They won't be starting north again till next April."

"I figgered maybe I could hire on this winter so's I could be a drover, come spring."

It was several minutes before the barber spoke again. "You ain't asked my advice, but iffen you did, I'd have to warn you about that. You'd best fight shy of them Texas herds."

"How come?"

"They're Johnny Rebs, for one thing."

John squinted narrowly. The wounds of the civil war were still deep. "For another?"

"Ain't you heard about that tick fever them longhorns been bringing north?"

He shook his head.

"Well, when them herds first started a-coming, nobody else had heard about them and the trouble they cause. We didn't mind much when they drove through Kansas on their way to Kansas City or St. Louis at first. But last year the cattle and livestock on both sides of the trail clean across Kansas died like flies after the big herds went north. It was that tick fever as killed them!" He aimed a stream of tobacco juice at the spittoon some distance away. "Now the ranchers and squatters is having meetings. They're a-fixing to stop them herds and turn them back, iffen they have to bring in hired guns to do it."

John hadn't had much contact with Texans, except for his pa and Waddy Ross, but the way he figured, stopping those herds would take some doing. "Sounds like big trouble," he said.

"That's what I'm a-telling you. So my advice is, get yourself a job back off the trail. Don't get into no fight that ain't none of your doing. There ain't no call to get yourself kilt in somebody else's row."

John fell silent till he was out of the chair and paying his bill.

"You really looking for work?" the barber asked at last.

Young Breckenridge nodded.

"Might not hurt to go over to see Bob Whittaker at the livery barn. He caught that hostler of his sleeping on the job a couple of weeks ago and fired him on the spot. The last I heard he hadn't found no one to take his place."

John thanked him and went out. He guessed he didn't have to get a job as a drover. All he really needed right now was work that would bring in a little money to get a room, something to eat, and clothes when he needed them. Perhaps it would be wise to go over and see this Mr. Whittaker. A job as a hostler would be a place to start, at least till he had a chance to find something else. There were ranchers around Abilene who might need a hand after he got to know them. If he could get on at the livery stable he wouldn't have to go all the way to Texas and risk getting into a fight when the herd reached Kansas.

Whittaker was on duty when Breckenridge approached him. Although they only talked a few minutes, the owner hired him.

"That horse of yours is in fine shape," Whittaker said. "The way I figger, anybody who'll take care of his own animal the way you're a-taking care of that sorrel ought to be good to have taking charge of other men's horses."

The boy went to work the following morning. He moved out of the hotel into Maggie Saunders' boardinghouse behind the stable where he was able to get a room he could afford. Several other young men had rooms at Maggie's place but John kept to himself. He was a loner, given to talking only when it was necessary. He preferred to spend his time in the barn currying the horses or in his room reading.

Young Breckenridge squirreled away every cent he could manage to save. By spring he was able to go down to the gunsmith's and buy a nickel-plated Smith and Wesson .32 caliber six-gun and holster, exactly like the one Lee Corbitt had gotten for him.

"You know how to use that?" the gunsmith demanded pointedly.

"A little."

"Around these parts, wearing one can get you into a pile of trouble you don't really need."

"I can take care of myself," he said hesitantly. "But I figger on getting better, soon as I've got a weapon to practice with."

"All right, I'll sell it to you. But don't say I didn't warn you."

10

In the days and weeks that followed John worked
out with the handgun at every opportunity, recall-
ing all that Corbitt had taught him and adding
innovations of his own. He soon realized that his
friend had been right when he said John had in-
herited his father's skills. He had been born with
a nimble hand and the sort of speed that could not
be acquired merely by practice. His moves were
silk-smooth and fast as lightning in a distant sky.
One instant his hand hovered near the weapon;
the next it was in his hand, out of the holster, and
pointed ominously at the target he had chosen.

He thought he would be able to practice behind the stable, but that was not to be. When
Whittaker saw the gun he explained the rules he
had set down several years before.

"You're old enough to know whether ya want
to carry that thing," he said. "And you can play
with it all you want, but I don't allow no shooting
around the barn. Remember that."

So John had to wait till he had time off to ride
out of town and practice. Even though he could
only manage that once or twice a week, he found
that his accuracy increased along with his speed.
He had a new confidence with each passing week.
Not that he was hankering to use the gun on

another man or that he longed to test his speed against an adversary; far from it. He saw the revolver as a defensive weapon; something he would use only if he had to.

Winter came and went; one frosty, snow-shrouded day after another. Work in the livery barn dropped off as business dwindled on the heels of the bitter cold and the snow piled high on the roads, making travel difficult. But Whittaker had promised John steady work and kept him on, although there were weeks when there was little for him to do.

As the days finally began to lengthen and the cold moderated, people resumed traveling. Soon the livery stable was comfortably filled and once more John had enough work to keep him busy. He was on duty just before dark one evening when he saw a well-muscled dun and an all-too-familiar bay come to a halt in front of the barn. He didn't see the bay's rider. He didn't have to. He knew who it was: Lee Corbitt, his old friend!

For a moment or two, time stood still. John remained motionless, robbed of strength by the sudden appearance of Corbitt. The men out front dismounted. He could see their chaps and the bottom half of their holsters hanging below dirty sheepskin coats. Their faces were hidden from view by the necks and heads of their horses, but that didn't matter. He would have known Corbitt's mount anywhere. The dun could belong to one of the Haynes brothers or Obed Metzner, but that didn't matter either. Lee Corbitt was the one who was after him.

The men and horses moved forward. They were coming in! John turned and went back into the barn. He wasn't wearing his gun, but Corbitt could send him after it. Then there would be a showdown between them and he didn't want that. Not with Corbitt.

He was no longer afraid to face his former friend, although the outlaw was reputed to be as dangerous as a rattlesnake when holding a six-gun. John had every confidence that he could handle himself in a shoot-out with anybody, but he didn't want trouble with the man who had saved his life. He would have dashed out the backdoor but Whittaker, who was on his way forward, met and stopped him. "Where do you think you're going?" he demanded. "There're some customers up there."

Desperation gleamed in the boy's eyes. "It's a man I don't want to see. I mean he's a man I don't want to see me."

"He ain't your pa, is he?"

John shook his head.

Right then Corbitt's familiar voice boomed, "Anybody here?"

"We'll be with you in a jiffy!" the owner called loudly. Then, directing his attention back to his youthful hostler, he lowered his voice. "Have trouble with him?"

"Bad trouble. He tried to make me stay with him, but I ran off."

Whittaker eyed him suspiciously. "You didn't steal nothing?"

"No, sir! And that's the pure truth."

"If you're scared to face a man, you oughta quit wearing that iron."

"I ain't scared of him! I . . . I just don't want trouble with him. It wouldn't be right. He saved my life!"

Whittaker put a hand on young Breckenridge's back and pushed him gently toward the rear door. "I'll take care of him."

John slipped through the opening and waited, leaning against the frame building. As soon as the outlaws left the livery stable, Whittaker came and got him. John knew his employer was curious about Corbitt but he asked nothing and the boy didn't volunteer any information. He couldn't bring himself to say anything to anyone about his friend and former companion—not even his kindly boss. In spite of the fact that Corbitt was the sort of man he was, he had saved John's life and had been good to the boy.

"Did they say how long they'd be around?" John asked.

The owner of the livery stable chuckled. "They allowed as how they was going over to the faro table at the Bull's Head Saloon and stay till they broke it."

"Then they'll be around a spell. . . . I . . . I'll never be able to stay outta his way."

"That faro table at the Bull's Head ain't the easiest to break, they tell me. I don't go down in the Lone Star District myself, but those who do say Malone runs a mean table. They may not be around as long as you think."

Young Breckenridge hesitated. Corbitt had often talked about gambling. He wasn't just a common, ordinary run-of-the-mill gambler. He'd handled a few tables for the house himself in his years of wandering. He just might give the Bull's Head houseman a hard run, staying in longer than Whittaker thought he could.

"I . . . I've got a favor to ask," John blurted.

"Like what?"

"Would you take over in the morning?" he asked, "or till Corbitt leaves town?"

Whittaker nodded. "I figgered on that. . . . But there's one more thing. Was you a-riding that sorrel when you had your run-in with your friend?"

"That I was. I've had him since before I left home."

"Then we'd best get him outta here. If that character sees him, he'll know you're around. Nobody who ever seen that gelding once would forget him."

John hadn't thought of that.

"I've got a barn at my place with a couple of stalls and some hay. You can keep him there for a spell, if you've a mind to."

John took Rusty out of the livery stable and rode him to Whittaker's. The town was beginning to come alive as he moved the big gelding. He passed several riders but they gave no indication they had even seen him.

The following morning when John came down for breakfast at Maggie Saunders', most of the boarders were already at the table. They must have been there for some time, talking excitedly about an incident that had happened the night before at the Bull's Head.

"Were you there, Joe?" one of the boarders demanded of another.

"Joe wouldn't be there," someone else said, grinning. "He *never* goes down on Texas Street."

"Almost never," Joe corrected. "I just happened to stop in for a couple of beers. I was no farther away than from me to you when it happened."

The others hitched their chairs closer to the table and leaned forward.

"All right," the spokesman continued. "Start at the beginning. Tell us all about it."

The bank clerk cleared his throat. He was enjoying his moment in the center of the stage. "Well, I was at this table having a beer when them two strangers come in and said they wanted to play faro."

"Yeah?" They waited for him to continue, but he paused momentarily.

"Malone told them he'd be glad to accommodate them with poker but he wasn't in the mood for faro right then, which was all right with them. All they wanted was some action and they didn't care how they got it."

"Go on."

"Well, you know Hap Malone. He runs the crookedest game in Kansas. When he seen them strangers was most as good as he was he started palming cards. It wasn't long till this here feller—I think someone said his name was Corbitt—caught him cheating."

"Then what happened?"

"Malone whipped out that little derringer he keeps for such emergencies, but he wasn't fast enough. He wasn't even able to pull the trigger before this Corbitt feller nailed him with a slug from that Colt Peacemaker he packs. That .45 tore a hole in Malone as big as your fist. They hardly had time to stretch him out on the floor before he cashed in."

For the first time John spoke. "What did they do with Corbitt? Throw him in jail?"

"It weren't his fault Malone was cheating. All Corbitt did was catch him at it. Malone even drew first—we all seen that—so there wasn't nothing anybody could do."

John settled back in the chair, thankful that Corbitt hadn't been killed or arrested.

"The onliest thing the marshal did was tell him and his friend that they'd better move on. A guy like Malone has friends and relations around here, and they're mostly the kind who wouldn't have no sleepless nights over shooting Corbitt in the back to get even."

At the usual time to go to work, John left the house and walked in the direction of the livery barn. Once he reached a place where he couldn't be seen from the weary, faded boardinghouse he changed directions and went to Whittaker's where he watered Rusty and spent more than an hour currying the big, barrel-chested sorrel. Toward noon he ventured back to the livery stable and learned that Corbitt and his companion had gone earlier that morning. They told Mr. Whittaker they were on their way to Dodge City.

The talk of organizing the farmers and ranchers to stop the Texas herds at the border continued all winter. There were several meetings, and two or three of the biggest and most powerful ranchers in that part of Kansas spoke darkly about hiring some fast-guns to come in and stop those Johnny Rebs south of Abilene at the border. Everyone was sure there was going to be a bloody war before the matter was settled. Strangely, though, as spring approached and the men got busy, the talk died. It was as though the Texas fever no longer existed.

Then the herds arrived from the south, beginning early in June. At the first sign of the longhorns, gray with ticks, the talk turned ugly. But it was mostly talk. There were several fights in and out of the saloons, and one hot-headed settler was stabbed by a drover in the Lone Star District after picking a row with him. For a time the situation was sticky and it looked as though there could be more serious trouble, but the marshal quieted the locals, the herds moved on, and the incidents were over.

Following the movement of every herd into the area, however, there was a wave of deaths among the livestock of those who lived on either side of the trail. The trouble continued to increase with the passage of each successive drive. Now John understood what the barber meant when he advised him to get a job other than herding cattle north.

He would probably have completely forgotten about signing on a trail drive if Whittaker had kept the livery barn. He liked the work and had begun to think about saving for a stable of his own some day. He enjoyed handling horses and, like his boss said, men soon learned how well he took care of their riding stock. He hadn't been at the barn a month when some of the most influential and particular ranchers and cowhands came in, asking him to care for their mounts personally. Then, late in June, Whittaker told him that he had sold the barn.

"My brother in St. Louis, the one who was here last month, has been wanting to get out here for several years," he said. "And my missus is a-getting lonely for her folks back east. Dave made me an offer on the livery barn and our house—the whole ball of wax—and we decided to take him up."

Suddenly nausea swept over John. "Will he be needing help?"

"That's the only thing I don't like about the deal. I tried to get him to keep you, John. I tried hard. Told him it'd be good for business to have

122

you here, that men come in a-asking for you 'cause you do such a good job. But he's got two boys of his own. He figgers the three of them can handle things without no help."

They would be coming, the owner of the barn said, in the middle of September. He wasn't making an announcement of the sale yet, but he wanted John to know right away so he could be looking for a job.

Young Breckenridge tried to get other work in Abilene but the only openings he could find were those of night clerk at a large hotel, or as dishwasher in the town's most prestigious café. Neither job appealed to him, yet the time for Whittaker's brother to arrive was drawing near. He was afraid he might have to take anything he could get.

It was then that Josiah Snyder came back into town on his way south. His herd had been one of the last to reach Abilene that summer. Now he was on his way home, having shipped his cattle to St. Louis where he sold them for a surprisingly good price.

John met Snyder when the burly Texas rancher stopped in to tell him he had just arrived on the train from St. Louis and wanted to pick up his saddle horse and chuck wagon in the morning.

"My boys are supposed to be in town waiting for me and the missus. I sent them a wire so they're expecting us today. They might stop by here any time to see iffen we made it. If they do, tell them that me and the missus will be at the hotel, and they should come over to the Bull's Head for a drink. I'll meet them there in about an hour."

The drovers rode in before John had finished

taking care of Snyder's own mount and the big team that pulled the chuck wagon. He hadn't thought about trying to hire on with the Texan while Snyder was there, but shortly after the rancher left the idea came to mind. When the drovers identified themselves and he had given them their boss's message, he asked if they needed any hands.

"You couldn't prove it by me," the tallest said. "You'd have to ask him."

"I'll do that," John promised. "Just as soon as I get off work."

It was almost two more hours before young Breckenridge finished his work and was able to leave. He was afraid he might not be able to find the Texan, but he went down into the Lone Star District to the Bull's Head where Snyder had said he would be waiting.

John hadn't been in a saloon on many occasions and felt uneasy pushing through the swinging doors. Waddy would have worked him over good if he caught him in a place like this. His stepfather would take a drink himself, now and again, but he had warned Fletch and John against it repeatedly. Still, the boy told himself, Waddy wasn't anywhere near and his ma was dead. He could do as he pleased.

John Breckenridge paused inside the door, looking about. There were a dozen or more tables scattered about the big room; at least half were already filled with drinking men and a few overdressed women. The Bull's Head had brought in a new dealer and a game was going on in the far corner. The well-dressed gambler was shuffling the cards, glancing from one to the other of his grim, hard-faced clientele. Most of the chips were

124

racked in front of him, indicating that his associates had not been as lucky as they had hoped. John wondered if this house gambler was any more skillful at palming cards than Malone. If he wasn't, he decided, he probably wouldn't last long. Smoke hung in a cloud over the tables and the long, ornate bar, and the music was loud and off key. But for all of that the saloon was quiet compared to what it would be in an hour.

He remained motionless, surveying the crowd. It was strange how easy it was to pick out the drovers from the drifters and wagon-train pilgrims. They were all dressed about the same, but there was an undefinable confidence in the lean, weathered faces of the Johnny Rebs from Texas, even in the way they sat at the tables. Broad-brimmed hats were pushed back on their heads and their lean frames were hard and muscular. But it was their eyes John noticed first; they had a cold, far-off look, as though they were used to peering across endless miles in the shimmering summer heat or the biting frost of late fall when the snow was upon the drive.

Josiah Snyder and his men were at one of the tables near the front. They had a bottle of whiskey and were talking in low tones. John sauntered over to them. He had already decided what he would say, but now that he was there he was hesitant to speak.

At last Snyder looked up. "What's with you, boy?" he demanded, contempt edging his voice. "Ain't you never seen a man drink?"

"I . . . I want to talk to you."

Snyder recognized him for the first time. "You're from the livery barn, ain't you?"

John acknowledged that he was.

"Anything wrong with our hosses?"

125

"Nope. I just want to talk."

Snyder's expression softened and he didn't seem quite so hostile. "What you want to talk about?"

"I'm looking for a job as a drover." John could feel the stranger's gaze piercing him.

"What's the matter? Lose yours?"

"The barn's been sold and the new owner's got boys of his own to do the work."

Josiah Snyder surveyed him critically. "You don't learn about cows at a livery barn."

John pulled himself erect. "I was born on a ranch, so I know cattle. I can haze and rope and brand as good as most any hand you've got."

"You sound mighty high on yourself."

"I'm telling the truth. That's what you want to hear, ain't it?"

The corners of the man's mouth narrowed and a smile softened his eyes. "Use a gun?"

John nodded.

"Good with it?"

"Tolerable."

He poured himself another drink. "I ain't got much work this winter, so I couldn't pay you very good till we start north in the spring. Say $8 a month and food."

"Sounds fair to me."

But Snyder hadn't yet made up his mind. "Tell you what you do. Come to the hotel tomorrow morning and have breakfast with me and the missus. We'll talk then."

When John arrived at the hotel the following morning, Josiah Snyder and his wife, Belle, were already in the dining room. She reminded the boy of his ma. Belle was a gaunt, spare woman, dressed in the plain cotton dress and high button shoes of the day. To see her, no one would have been aware that she was on her way home after being on the trail since early April, supervising the cook and giving a hand with the hazing when she was needed. She seemed to have the endurance and vigor of a sturdy, straight-limbed pine. Yet the savage, debilitating summer had taken its toll, along with other years just as difficult. John supposed she was some years younger than her husband, though she appeared to be older. The West had a way of doing that to women. Her graying hair was pulled severely back over her head and fashioned in a bun at the nape of her neck, accentuating the lines about her eyes and the corners of her mouth.

Only her eyes remained young, untouched by the hardships and uncertainties of the Civil War years and the constant battle with the elements and the Indians who roamed their section of Texas. They were soft and brown and lights danced nimbly in them when she laughed. Almost immediately he decided he liked her. And she seemed to like him.

That meant a great deal to Snyder. As soon as he noted Belle's reaction to the new hand he was considering telling John he could use him. The job wouldn't pay much in the winter when there was little to do, but when they started putting the herd together young Breckenridge would get $25 a month.

"But you get nothing if ya quit on the way. Understand?"

"I understand."

"OK. Go get your gear and your horse. We'll be a-leaving in an hour."

Excitement and relief surged through the young drover. He had a job!

11

John rushed back to the livery stable, collected his wages, and saddled Rusty. After a brief stop at the boardinghouse to pay his bill and pick up his things, he was ready to leave. Belle Snyder was on the chuck wagon when he returned, the reins in her hands.

"Wouldn't you like to have me tie my horse behind and drive for you, Ma'am?" he asked.

She stiffened primly. "And why would I want you to do that?"

"No reason, except you look tired."

"Oh, pshaw!" she rejected his suggestion with a quick wave of her hand. "I was driving horses before you was born. Ain't nothing about driving a team to make a body tired. . . . Now when Josiah and me came out from Georgia in '57, I had to walk mostly." Her smile was bright and warm. "Now that's what I call tiring."

He touched the brim of his hat and rode a few paces away. The Texas rancher came out of the livery barn presently, leading his own horse. Mike Wahl and a young drover who went by the name of Stub Cooper were close behind.

"Let's get on the road!" Snyder growled, swinging into the saddle. He led the little procession south with the chuck wagon in the middle and the drovers following. They camped on the bank of the Salt Fork Four that night and forded the wagon to the other side early in the morning. When they finished and were taking a brief rest, Josiah went over to John.

"Whittaker at the livery stable gave you quite a recommend," he said. "Told me you was the best hostler he'd ever had."

John's cheeks darkened with embarrassment. "I'm right obliged to him."

The smile faded from the burly moustached rancher's lips. "While you're a-working for me I expect you to live up to what he said. I ain't got no room for any other kind of drovers. Understand?"

It took them more than three weeks to reach the Walking S near Tucupido in west Texas some distance below the tick-free area of the southern state. John had thought it hot in Abilene during the summer, but as they traveled he realized he hadn't even known what heat was. Although the hottest time of year had passed and they were approaching fall, the flaming sun withered everything in sight. The grassland was as dry as the bark on a twisted, dying mesquite; even the cacti and yucca were pale and sickly, as though they had decided that survival was not worth the struggle. The water holes, fed by springs that trickled feebly through the rocks and sandy clay, had shrunk to a fraction of their former size. On two occasions the little band of travelers had to press on well into the night to reach another water source big enough to supply their needs.

Even though Josiah Snyder had told John there would be little for him to do during the winter, he found plenty of work around the Walking S. There were corrals to build and repairs to do on the barn. And when that was done there were always strays to rope and brand—longhorns as wild as the mountain lions that stalked their young.

It wasn't rustling. The ancestors of that sturdy breed may have belonged to somebody once, but those that roamed the Snyder spread and the surrounding ranches and government land had never been owned by anybody. They belonged to whoever had the courage to go into the mesquite and cacti after them. These cowhands who were reckless enough to drop a lariat over those mammoth horns and undertake to throw and brand their owner, could claim him. In John's case he was riding for the Walking S, so the longhorns he roped belonged to Snyder. And that was all right with him. If he ever had cattle, he wanted tame blood so it didn't risk a man's neck every time he worked them.

Young Breckenridge rode with Wahl most of the time. The older man usually did the roping, but it took two to throw the big brutes and do the branding. Even then it was a risky, tiring business that allowed no room for error. Those ugly beasts had sharp curved horns that were weapons worthy of their hostile dispositions. Make one small mistake like failing to hog-tie the bull properly, or not moving quickly enough once he was released, and he'd ram a hole as big as a fist into the cowboy's belly.

But as the herd grew steadily and the numbers of cattle increased, so did the scope of Snyder's plans. He had been conservative in the size of the herds he had taken north on two previous occasions, preferring to risk only the money he had at hand. Now, however, he was talking about getting together the biggest herd he had ever put on the trail.

"John," he said one Sunday when Belle had invited the boy in for dinner, "while you was in Abilene, did you ever hear talk about that so-called Texas or tick fever?"

"There was some talk," he acknowledged, "but nothing ever came of it."

"What kind of talk?"

"Some of the ranchers and settlers tried to get organized so as they could stop the herds before they got into Kansas—with their rifles if there weren't no other way."

Snyder pulled thoughtfully at one end of his moustache. "Reckon they'd do that?" he asked. "Especially when they know we'd be a-shooting back?"

John shrugged. "That's the way they was a-talking."

A minute or more passed as they sat at the table. Belle got up and poured coffee for the three of them.

"They might be spoiling for a fight," Snyder continued, "but I don't reckon they've got all that much stomach for real trouble. They'll do a lot of talking, but not much else till the state legislature gets around to passing a law against our herds coming into Kansas."

"If there is such a thing as tick fever," Belle asked, "why don't our cattle come down with it?"

"That's what I say." Snyder answered. "They got ticks all over them. Millions of ticks. But it don't slow them down none. They're healthy as any Missouri mule you ever did see."

"I can't say as I like the looks of all them bugs, fat with blood, a-hanging all over our cattle, but, pshaw, they don't seem to hurt nothing," she went on.

John listened intently. He had heard Kansas ranchers voice the opposite opinion. They said the cattle from Texas brought the fever with them and spread it wherever they went.

"I've been pondering what to do," the rancher went on. "I figger we got one or maybe two more years to drive north. Then them scatter-brained Yanks is a-going to pass laws against us."

"What, then?" Belle asked.

"We won't be able to get our herds into Kansas or on to Chicago where the real market is." He finished his coffee and held out the cup for his wife to fill it. "I reckon I'd like to get our share. . . . I was in Tucupido yesterday a-talking to old Powell in the bank. Been thinking of borrowing as much as I can on the Walking S and putting all of it into cattle. I'll drive them up to Abilene and we'll ship them to Chicago. We'll make it before they get around to passing laws against us."

Dismay flecked Belle's eyes. "You think that's wise, Josiah?" she asked.

The broad-shouldered rancher straightened deliberately and stared at her, anger distorting his heavy face. "If I didn't think it was wise, woman," he snapped, "I wouldn't do it!" She looked quickly away.

Once Snyder made his decision to take a final herd to St. Louis, a new, fevered energy seemed to have control over the Walking S. Before the week was out he had brought in a dozen new and eager young drovers, some from as far away as the Brazos. Most were Texans but there was a sprinkling of dark-skinned vaqueros among them—drovers with Mexican saddles, rawhide riatas, and the reckless courage that was their heritage.

Snyder put some of the new men out in the brakes searching for wild stuff to rope and subdue. At times the wild cattle could be lured into the open by small herds of decoys—tamer cows that could be herded near the brushy creek bottoms and stands of mesquite that provided sanctuary for their wild relatives. But that ruse only worked with a few. Most had to be cut from the protection of their thorny hiding places at dawn, while they were grazing, and that was not easy.

The rider plunged into the prickly, razor-sharp bush without regard for himself or his mount as he followed the nimble-footed bull that could run like a jackrabbit. When he got close enough he had to lay a loop over the critter, throw a double half-hitch about the saddle horn, and jerk the stubborn animal off his feet. Then, while the bull was being held on a tight rope, the rider leaped from the saddle, snatched the pigging string from around his waist, and hog-tied the struggling brute. It was a dangerous, intriguing game that set the drover's heart to racing and challenged his daring and skill. Though most men admitted their fear, they kept at it day after day.

Once the beast was securely tied, the drover usually had a smoke and waited, allowing the longhorn to battle against the bonds until he was too stiff to run fast or far. Then he was released and driven to the herd. Even then, he wasn't defeated and had to be constantly watched by the men to keep him from breaking away to return to his old haunts.

While these activities were going on, Snyder took several other riders with him to bring back the cattle he bought. Some ranchers in the area, not far from the Walking S, regularly sent their hands south to raid the Mexican spreads. It was comparatively easy to pick up two or three hundred head on a raid with little danger of being caught. Once they were on the American side of the border, few Mexicans dared to go after them. But that was not Snyder's way; he got his cattle legally or not at all.

At the time the hands were working hard to build up the herd, Belle was preparing for the long trip to Abilene. She came out to the bunkhouse one morning and insisted that John help her. She was going to Tucupido for supplies. He hesitated, knowing the hands still in the bunkhouse were watching with obvious amusement. "I was a-going with Mike to look for wild stuff."

"He can get someone else." With that she swished hurriedly toward the house and he followed. Once inside she had him sit down. "Take that pencil and write what I tell you." He stared curiously at her.

She saw the question in his eyes and laughed. "I was too busy a-helping Ma with the babies that came along every year to learn to read and write."

"I'm powerful sorry," he said lamely.

"Pshaw! It don't matter. Josiah can read and write real good. He reads out loud of an evening when he's a mind to. And if I need something writ and he ain't here, you can do it for me." She sat across from him as though they had already wasted too much time. "Now, put this down. Three bags of flour. One sack of sugar. One of beans. A big bag of coffee. Two tins of lard . . . ," her voice droned on.

He realized, then, that she didn't need a list. She had locked every item fast in her nimble mind and was not likely to forget anything. Still, he had to keep writing. When he finished recording the long list of staples that would be needed to feed the hungry drovers on the first stretch of the drive, she had him read the items back to her. Everything was in order.

"I'll go harness the team for you," he said, getting to his feet.

Her eyes gleamed the way they did when she was amused. "Didn't I tell you? I want you to go to town with me." He knew better than to argue.

On the way he learned the purpose of his being with her. "I've told Josiah to get a cook who didn't need watching for this trip," she said. "I ain't a-going."

His eyes widened. "I though you *always* went."

"I have . . . until now." Her face sobered.

"Is something *wrong*?"

She laid a hand on his muscular young arm. "That's why I had you come along. I've got to talk to you." He waited uneasily.

"I ain't said nothing to Josiah," she began. "It'd only worry him, but I've been ailing some since we got back from the drive last fall."

The spectre of his mother's thin, emaciated face leaped to mind. "What is it, Belle?"

"I don't know for sure, but I'm always tired. . . . It's like nothing I've ever had before. I hardly got the strength to get up of a morning. I know I'd only be in the way." She managed a thin smile. "I've been a-telling myself it'll get better soon, but I keep on feeling right poorly. There's no use in my even thinking I could go north."

"Have you seen the doc?"

She shook her head.

"You oughta do that, Belle. An you oughta tell Josiah. He's got a right to know."

"*I can't!* He's borrowed all that money and bought cattle. If he knew, he might stay home. . . . Then where'd we be?" For a time they traveled in silence.

"I don't know whether Josiah ever told you or not, but our son, Jared, would be about your age iffen he'd lived through the fever. He died when he was two."

John had not known they ever had a son.

"I think that might be one reason he hired you—because he thought about our boy. . . ." She cleared her throat. "In the few months you've been with us he's come to think a lot of you."

"He's a good boss."

"You're more than just a drover to him."

"I . . . I think a lot of him, too." He was embarrassed by the turn of the conversation, though he strongly suspected that what she said was true.

"That's why I . . . I wanted to talk to you. I've been a-worrying about what'd happen to him if . . . if he comes home and . . . and I wasn't here."

"Don't talk that way!" John exclaimed sharply.

"Pshaw, John. There's probably nothing to it and I'll live to be ninety. It's just that I . . . I'd feel a sight better about the herd going without me if I knowed you was a-going to be around to take care of him. For awhile, anyway."

"I'll stay," he promised, "iffen he wants me to."

She smiled gratefully. "Now, don't say nothing about this little talk of ours."

"If that's the way you want it," he replied, trying to ignore the growing uneasiness that swept over him.

"That's the way I want it."

He was uncomfortable around Josiah in the days that followed. He knew he should tell his boss and friend the real reason Belle wasn't going with them. Yet she had sworn him to secrecy and he could not break his word. He was boxed in and he didn't like it. Grimly he tried to force those thoughts aside. For some reason he didn't quite succeed.

12

The herd continued to grow as the first of April came and went. Still, Snyder didn't have all the cattle he wanted before starting north. The new hands were getting restive, and the experienced drovers were concerned.

John had never worked on a drive before, but he had lived in Abilene long enough to know they ought to be on their way. The drovers and ranchers who came around the livery barn always said it was important to get an early start. He and Mike Wahl talked it over and decided they should confront their employer in an effort to get him to see the importance of leaving immediately.

"Mr. Snyder," the trail boss said when they approached him, "we're a-losing way too much time. That trail's a-going to be clogged with herds by the time we get close to Kansas. Summer'll be a-getting on and the grass'll be as short as the hair on a bull frog's nose . . . and it'll feed our cows just about as well."

"When I was a-living in Abilene," John put in, "they told me the best trail bosses got started north by April first."

Snyder had been sitting at the kitchen table drinking coffee when they came in. For two minutes after they had spoken he stared at the wall, eyes narrowing and cheeks flushing angrily.

"Are you trying to tell me I don't know my own business?" he demanded harshly.

"We're a-trying to tell you we've got to get on the trail if you ever want to see that herd to market!" Wahl snorted, as angry and irritable as his boss. "I got a bunch of drovers that're getting mighty all-fired hard to handle. They're ornery as them longhorn bulls on the prod. I don't know how long I can keep the lid on."

"I can always get a new trail boss," Snyder said sternly, "iffen you don't think you can handle them."

"It ain't that! I'm just a-saying, let's go. If we ain't a-going, let's fire three-fourths of them fellers and send them home."

Before Josiah could reply, Belle came in, smiling brightly. "I'll bet you boys come in for a cup of coffee."

"They come in because they don't think I'm a-taking care of things to suit them," her husband snapped. "I'm about to send them both packing!"

She poured coffee for Wahl and John and sat down across from her husband. Gently she placed her hand over his.

"Now, Josiah," she said softly. "You know that ain't why they're here. They're just concerned because they want to get on the trail."

"I'll say when we leave. I won't have my men a-telling me!"

"I know that. And they do, too. But I've heard you say more than once that nobody oughta leave these parts with a herd any later than early April. That's what's eating on Mike and John. You're going agin what you taught them."

He held out his cup, wordlessly, and she went to the stove for the coffeepot.

"I know we're getting a late start," he said, his manner softening, "and we oughta be on the trail by now. But this's my *last* chance to get in on that big Eastern money. I've got to make it now or I'll *never* make it!" He got to his feet. "Sit on them drovers for another ten days, Mike. By that time we'll be on our way, even if I ain't been able to add another cow to our herd."

That didn't really suit the trail boss but it was the best they could do. "Sounds all right, Mr. Snyder."

But holding the drovers in check wasn't as simple as Snyder made it sound. As long as they were spending long, hard hours in the saddle searching the brakes for cattle or moving the herd to new grass, there were no problems. But they had cleaned the longhorns out of their area to the point where it was no longer profitable to keep looking, and the cattle had just been moved to a new pasture. There was only work for a few at one time, riding the perimeter of the big herd and keeping it together.

There were several flare-ups between the white drovers and the Mexican vaqueros that were mostly words and a few isolated punches. There was no real trouble until two days before they were to leave. Snyder had come in that morning at breakfast and given the word that they were about ready to move out.

That ignited the desire in some of the men to have one last fling before the dusty, tiring days on the trail. They knew they could not get time off to go into town, so they did the next best thing. As soon as John and Wahl left the bunkhouse somebody sneaked in to Tucupido for several bottles of whiskey. By the time the trail boss came back, the men were getting loud and belligerent. John, who had come in shortly after the drinking began and was lying on his bunk, had the uneasy feeling that something was about to happen, but there was nothing he could do about it.

Even then, there might not have been trouble, had it not been for the poker game that was in progress. One of the white drovers lost more than he thought he should have and accused the Mexican dealer of cheating.

"You say I cheat, Señor?" the vaquero growled viciously. "You lie!"

Barlow's face purpled. "There ain't no greaser a-calling *me* no liar!"

The vaqueros in the bunkhouse began to gather behind their compadre, their manner hostile and menacing.

"If you say I cheat, you lie!" he repeated recklessly.

John Breckenridge had been watching the progress of the game and saw the fight coming, but he waited for Wahl to stop it. After all, he was the trail boss.

Either Wahl didn't recognize the seriousness of the situation or had tired of keeping the men in line, but he did nothing. Barlow reached impulsively across the table, his fingers seeking the vaquero's throat. In an instant the Mexican whipped out a knife and lunged for him.

Then the trail boss sprang into action. He saw the gleaming blade a split second before it struck its target and he shoved the drover out of the way. The knife missed its intended victim and caught Wahl in the shoulder. It was razor sharp and sliced into his body, up to the hilt.

With that, the Texans leaped on the vaqueros,

fists swinging. A blow caught the dealer and sent him sprawling backward into a bunk, hitting his head. The Mexicans jerked out their knives, and for a brief instant John was afraid that even more would be hurt. And nobody seemed to be doing anything to stop it!

He whipped out his gun and fired twice into the ceiling. That restored a measure of reason. The fighting stopped, at least for the moment.

"We've had enough of this!" he snapped with authority.

"Says who?" a surly Texan demanded.

Young Breckenridge faced him, his eyes cold. "I do," he answered quietly. "Want to make something of it?"

"I don't think you're *man* enough to make that stick!" It was a direct challenge—the first time John had faced one.

An icy smile lifted the corners of his mouth, mirthlessly. "Try me!"

In that moment the drover saw that he was deadly serious and backed off. "You can say that. I ain't wearing a gun."

"We can take care of that right now, if you've a mind to." The drover moved back and the challenge was over.

John glanced at the trail boss. Wahl was sitting on a bunk, a handkerchief to his shoulder, trying to stop the flow of blood.

"You two," John ordered quickly, "take care of Mike. . . . The rest of you come over to the table, one at a time, and put down your knives."

The vaqueros glared at him and did not respond.

"Move!"

"No, Señor!" the self-styled spokesman

exclaimed, putting his hand on the handle of his own knife. "We keep."

"Not and work for the Walking S, you don't! Bring them knives over here. We're not having anybody else hurt." They began to talk excitedly among themselves.

By this time Belle and Josiah Snyder had reached the bunkhouse. They had heard the shots and rushed out.

Belle saw that Wahl had been badly injured and that two of the drovers had cut away his shirt and were trying to stop the bleeding.

"Here," she said crisply as John explained what happened. "Let me do that." She realized the wound was a bad one and ordered one of the men to the house for flour.

"How much?"

"Just get me flour! Plenty of it."

". . . So, we had a little ruckus," John was concluding to Josiah, "but it's under control now."

"You sure?"

He nodded.

The drover came hurrying back, a sack of flour on his shoulder.

"Open it!" Belle ordered. Without waiting for him to do so she loosed the strings that closed the sack and began to put flour on the open wound, packing it in place as the blood moistened it.

"Hurt much?" she asked Wahl.

"It's tolerable."

About that time the vaqueros approached Snyder. "You pay us now, Señor," the spokesman said. "OK?"

"The month ain't over yet. I pay at the end of the month. Understand?"

The Mexican shook his head. "No, Señor. You pay now. We leave."

Snyder turned toward John. "What's this all about?"

John's cheeks tinged with color. "I'm afraid I fired them!"

"You *what*?" Josiah exploded.

"I told them to put their knives on the table so we wouldn't have no more trouble. When they wouldn't do it I said if they didn't, they were fired."

Snyder turned that over in his mind.

"It was the only thing I could do. I was afeared somebody'd be hurt bad."

Snyder nodded. "With Wahl out of commission somebody had to take charge."

He told the vaqueros to come to the house where he paid them the wages they had earned. Silently they filed out of the frame building and rode off.

"Now I suppose we'd best get Wahl to Tucupido to the doctor," he told John.

"I'll harness the team."

". . . And maybe you'd best come along. You and me have got a job on our hands a-hiring new drovers."

"Why me?" John asked.

"The trail boss *always* wants to have a look at his new men before they're hired."

He still did not understand. "Trail boss?"

"Yeah. With Wahl hurt and not able to make the drive, I've got to have a new trail boss. From what happened in the bunkhouse a little while ago, you're the one for the job."

"But I ain't never been on a drive," he protested. "I've worked cattle plenty but I don't know nothing about handling a trail drive."

"You know how to handle men. That's the

main thing," Snyder told him. "I'll be along. I can help with taking them across rivers and the like."

After leaving Wahl at the doctor's office, Snyder and John Breckenridge made the rounds of the saloons in an effort to hire more drovers to take the places of the Mexican vaqueros who had been fired. Snyder had gone a long way to pick up drovers before, but now he was in a hurry so he tried to get local men. They had little success, however.

"I tell ya, Josiah," the bartender in the El Centro Saloon said, "there ain't hardly nobody around who's a-looking for work. Some of them big outfits from down east was through three or four weeks ago—right after you hired your boys. They scooped up about everybody who looked like they could straddle a horse."

"We've got a passel of them no account longhorns that's been running wild since the day they was born," the rancher explained. "And we've got to have ourselves eight or ten more drovers or we'll be stringing cattle all the way from here to Abilene."

The bartender finished wiping the glasses and leaned forward on the polished mahogany.

"Them big boys wasn't all that keen on a-picking up Mex drovers. Have you tried the south end?"

Snyder hesitated.

"It was vaqueros we had trouble with. I'd as soon get along without them."

"They're the onliest ones I can think of."

Finally Snyder and Breckenridge went down to the Mexican section of Tucupido and tried to hire men to help move the herd north. However, word of the trouble at the Snyder ranch had preceded them. Although there seemed to be plenty of idle men around, none of them wanted to work for the Walking S.

"What're we gonna do?" John asked.

"We'll get them if we have to go all the way to San Antone," Snyder muttered darkly.

The rancher turned in at the Sombrero Saloon and made his way to the bar. John followed. There were a number of men in the adobe building, sitting at the tables or standing at the battered counter. Young Breckenridge recognized two of them as vacqueros who had left earlier that day.

"You look for somebody, Señor?" the dark-skinned bartender asked.

Snyder nodded. "About eight or ten men who want to earn good money riding for me."

The Mexican took a step to one side and raised his voice. "Anybody here want to work for Señor Snyder?"

A taut silence fell over the squalid, dimly-lighted room. The men glared at the rancher and his young companion.

"The pay's good!" Snyder cried. "And I treat my men good. Ask anybody who's ever ridden for me." He glanced about. "You, Hernandez!" He pointed to a leathery, hard-faced vaquero who must have been forty but looked to be sixty. "You've been on drives with me. You know I pay your people the same as white drovers and I treat them good."

Deliberately, Hernandez got to his feet, picked up his chair and turned so his back was to the rancher. The conversation at the tables began again and the rancher and his trail boss were completely ignored. Impulsively Snyder grasped the bartender by the arm.

"Know where I can find any vaqueros?"

He shrugged expressively. "Maybe up the street. Maybe not!"

Snyder frowned his displeasure. "What's the matter with them, anyway? I had nothing to do with the fight in my bunkhouse today."

"They have ears, Señor," the bartender retorted blandly. "And they can talk. Ask them."

By then Snyder realized it was hopeless to try to persuade any of the Mexicans in Tucupido to come and work for him. None of them would set foot on the Walking S in spite of the fact that, until that day, his record with them had been good.

"I've gotta get out of here before I lose my temper," he muttered under his breath.

When they were out on the dusty street once more, John turned to his employer. "What now?"

Snyder thought for a minute. "Ain't no use trying here. They're a proud people and they don't take too kindly to being accused of cheating. . . . Even if they was, they don't like being caught. I could ring Barlow's neck!"

John's gaze met his. "I suppose I'm the one they've got it in for."

They mounted and slowly rode north. It was several minutes before Snyder spoke again.

"I've been doing some thinking, Breckenridge. There ain't no drovers left around here and we ain't got a chance of getting no vaqueros from Tucupido this year. Go home and keep an eye on things. And tell Belle I'm a-heading east a-looking for men. I'll be back when I've got them."

13

It was almost a week before Snyder returned with six white drovers and four Mexicans. They were a sorry lot—ragged and shifty-eyed—men who would have looked more at home in jail than on the trail.

"I know they don't look like much," he said, defensively, "but they claim to know longhorns and they was all I could get."

The new men didn't have long to settle in at the Walking S. They spent one day on the ranch, and the following morning before dawn they moved out, urging the big herd to start north.

The herd was still a surging, shapeless, stubborn mass, but when it was finally broken in and trail-wise, it would assume a semblance of order and move with slow, methodical moves.

John would ride out first with the chuck wagon behind him. The wrangler would drive the remuda to one side, far enough away so the horses wouldn't spook the herd. Two of the best and most reliable drovers would ride point, one on either side of the lead cows. Behind them the men riding swing and flank would keep the reluctant and ill-tempered longhorns in line. Following the last stragglers, half a dozen drovers would ride drag.

Josiah would be riding at John's side when they were on the trail, but now he seemed reluctant to leave. Belle stood near the corral, watching him saddle his horse.

"You sure you won't change your mind about going along?" he asked hopefully.

"Not this time."

"What's so different about this time?" he asked, his eyes narrowing.

"We've gone all over that before," she told him.

He knew, even before he asked, that she would not relent. That was the way she was. There was no use in talking. She wasn't going to change. He took her in his arms for a moment before mounting and riding off to catch the others.

The first days of a cattle drive were always difficult. Those wild, shifty-eyed critters were as cunning as the wolves that roamed the hills; they were as tough as the rawhide riatas of the vaqueros and stubbornly resistant to being moved off their range. As a result, cows and bulls alike were constantly bolting, taking off for the mesquite thickets that offered a measure of concealment.

The men spent long, sweaty, dusty hours in the saddle, working desperately to get the herd started toward Abilene. Bodies were exhausted and tempers frayed by the time a cantankerous old lineback cow decided to take charge of the situation. She was a dusty ebony with a white stripe from the nape of her powerful neck to the base of her tail—an ill-tempered critter with horns set close together and curved outward to kill.

She stopped grazing suddenly and lifted her head like a doughty old monarch about to assume command of the armies and lead them into battle. She struck out for the lead position and Kansas, as surely as though she had examined a map herself. Her long, lean legs propelled her rapidly over the rough ground, and, dutifully, those less strong-minded than she, bowed to her leadership and followed behind her. The herd began to assume its classic form and move more rapidly.

That did not mean the drovers' troubles were behind them. Most of the longhorns were still wild and stubborn. One would dart out from the surging mass of cattle, horns lowered dangerously, and six or more would follow. Their hooves pounded the hard, dry ground, and they kept a wicked eye out for the drovers whom they sensed would be after them. The third day out one of the men had a horse gored under him and was thrown, breaking a leg.

Snyder swore when he saw him. "I wish Belle were here. She knows how to take care of things like that."

"We'd better get him to a doctor," John said.

The older man's eyes were dark with anger, as though the drover had deliberately caused the accident. "Can't spare no one to take him anywhere," he said. "We'll get Cookie to have a look at him. He's been on a lot of drives, and he's helped out with patching up drovers when there ain't no doc around."

"But we ain't that far from a doc. I can have him to town and be back in half a day."

Snyder scowled. "That's half a day we ain't got to spare. It's not my fault he was so clumsy he got his leg busted." His voice raised. "We've got us a herd to move!"

But young Breckenridge stood his ground.

"We can't leave him go. His leg's got to be took care of right or he could have a limp all his life."

"Don't try to tell me what I've got to do!" Snyder exploded. "I don't *have* to do nothing."

"As long as I'm trail boss I'm a-taking care of my men!"

"Keep that up and you won't be trail boss!"

John's eyes narrowed coldly. "Any time you want to make a change, it's all right with me."

He turned on his heel and hurried back to the place where the injured rider was lying. The man's face was wet with sweat, and his body was beginning to tremble.

"Couldn't find no one to set this leg, could ya?" he asked, concern creeping into his voice.

"I'm taking ya to town," John said. "They tell me Victoria ain't far."

"I heard Snyder," Kramer retorted, gritting his teeth against the numbing pain. "You ain't a-taking me nowhere's."

"It don't make no difference what he says! You was riding for the Walking S and I'm taking care of you the way I'd want to be taken care of if I had a busted leg."

John hadn't heard the owner of the herd come up behind him until he spoke. "It don't make no difference what *who* says?" Josiah demanded, pointedly.

"It don't make no difference what *anybody* says!" John repeated. "I already told you that. I take care of my men."

"You do what I say," Snyder reminded him hotly. "You work for me!"

John raised his gaze to meet that of his employer. He didn't want trouble with Josiah but he couldn't leave Kramer without having a doctor set that leg.

"I know I work for you, but Kramer's got to get to a doc. If you feel you've got to fire me for it, go ahead!"

Their eyes met. For a long minute the rancher's heavy, florid features contorted with rage. Then he shrugged in resignation. "Just see that ya get back here, soon as ya can. OK?"

John caught up Rusty and a quiet, gentle mare that would be likely to give the injured man an easy time. Then he got Cookie to splint the leg securely so the injury wouldn't be made worse on the ride. Sweat moistened the drover's shirt and his face was ashen by the time the splinting was finished.

"Feeling all right?" John asked him.

"Tolerable."

The young trail boss knew that wasn't true. He changed his plan. "We can't take ya to town on horseback. I'll have to go for the doc."

He mounted his big sorrel and rode off, conscious of the fact that Snyder was staring belligerently after him.

It was almost dark when John rode back to the place where Snyder had bedded the herd down for the night. "Doc's right behind me with his buggy," he told Kramer. "How ya feeling?"

"Not so good."

"He'll have ya fixed up in no time."

At that moment the rancher approached. "I want to talk to you, Breckenridge!" he snapped.

John pulled the saddle from Rusty's back and turned his horse into the remuda before directing his attention to his boss. Snyder led him some distance from the chuck wagon and the drovers who were gathered around it.

"Ya got away with this because I'd have to

face Belle when I got back home if I fired ya. She wouldn't take too kindly to that. But, no matter what she says, don't go agin me no more! Iffen you do, you're through. That's a promise."

John did not back down. "I don't like going agin you. I'm beholden for everything you and Belle have done for me. But I've got to take care of my men. You let me do that and we'll get along fine!"

The older man grasped his arm with iron fingers. "Remember what I told you!"

Young Breckenridge jerked away. "Don't ever lay a hand on me again."

Snyder cursed under his breath and stalked off.

John went back to where the doctor was working on the injured Kramer. The doc set the leg and made a plaster cast for it.

"It's a good thing you didn't try to bring him in town on horseback the way you planned," Doc said to John when he finished. "The break's a bad one. You'd have scrambled things good if you'd put him on a horse for a ride like that."

The rancher came over just then and paid the doctor for the visit.

"Don't know what we're going to do with him," he muttered. "He's sure enough going to be in the way till that leg heals."

The doctor's mouth tightened. "You'll have to fix a place for him in the chuck wagon. He can't ride a horse and ya can't leave him out here, that's for sure."

For the next week or more, things were cool between the owner of the herd and his trail boss. Snyder spoke to John only when he had to and John kept out of his way as much as possible.

There were no more arguments between them, but the hostility was thinly veiled.

At the same time, the drovers were increasingly cordial to Breckenridge. Until Kramer broke his leg some of the older hands had resented his youth and lack of experience.

"We'd as well not have a trail boss!" they had told each other, not always careful to wait until he was out of hearing before they spoke. But when he defied the rancher to go to town for the doctor, that changed.

"He stood up to Snyder!" those same drovers exclaimed, admiration in their voices. "He stood up to him."

"That kid's got a lot of sand."

From then on it was easier for John to get things done. The older men began helping him when they saw that he needed the benefit of their experience. The herd started to move faster and there were fewer problems on the trail. As Snyder saw that, his ill temper thawed. By the time they neared the Kansas border south of Abilene, something of their formerly warm relationship had been restored.

The herd was two days from the border when a tall, weathered Texan on his way south stopped to spend the night with them. He had wintered in Colorado to try his hand at prospecting for gold in the spring. Now he was on his way home, his pockets empty and his disillusionment great.

"Some men are striking it rich," he admitted in answer to their questions over a scalding cup of black coffee. "But not me. All I got was a sore back."

"I been a-thinking I'd like to try my hand at prospecting some day," John told him.

"Take it from me. It ain't what people says it is."

After supper the rancher got John and the Texan aside. "You come through Abilene," he said to the stranger, "what's it like up there? For the trail herds, I mean."

"Rough."

"I've been afeared of that."

"I was there last year," John said. "There was talk then of getting everybody together to keep the herds from Texas out on account of the fever."

"As near as I can see, that's just what they've done. Them Yankee ranchers and sod busters has finally got together. They tell me they're a-meeting the herds at the border around Caldwell with rifles and six-guns." He drained his cup and poured out the grounds. "They're a-saying the herds can go west and give tick fever to the buffalo."

Snyder breathed deeply. He had gambled against those stubborn Yanks being able to agree on anything. Now it sounded as though he was in real trouble. If it were just guns they'd be facing he wouldn't give that a thought; he'd faced his share of guns during the war. But how could they keep a herd of longhorns together and fight at the same time? Especially if the other side brought in gunfighters?

"Any hired hands helping them?" he asked.

"No Texans. We don't turn on our own. But they tell me there's plenty of strangers around Abilene and has been all spring. My guess is they've brought in some hired guns. Wouldn't know how many."

The stranger had supper with Snyder and John, spent the night, and ate breakfast before continuing his journey south. When he was gone the rancher told John he wanted him to go along to town.

"The men can handle the herd," he said. "I figger you and me have got to get in to Caldwell and see what things is like. If there's going to be bad trouble, I'd like to know about it."

They saddled up and rode off together. They had been on the trail an hour when John asked a question that had tormented him since their guest from Texas told them about the possibility of trouble.

"You've hired some of these men before," he said. "If push comes to shove, will they be with us, or will they turn tail and run?"

"They work for the brand," Snyder said confidently. "If the bullets start a-flying they'll be with us all the way."

The grubby little town of Caldwell, Kansas, was in view, an ugly scab on the trail ahead, when they could see the tell-tale plume of dust sent up by a group of riders coming out from town.

"Appears we're a-going to have company," Snyder said, unfastening the thong on his gun. John did the same.

"Think they're coming because of us?" he asked.

"Why else? They know we're here. They've seen the dust put up by the herd."

The two men rode forward calmly. A strange sensation took hold of John—a tense expectancy that set every nerve in his body to tingling. He wondered if his pa had ever felt this way when he was about to face a man in a gun battle.

The riders from town were pushing their mounts hard and in a few minutes were close enough for Snyder and young Breckenridge to count nine men.

"That don't make good odds," Snyder warned. "Be careful, John. There's got to be some dangerous men among them."

The strangers spread out as they approached. One man stopped slightly in front of the others, leaving no doubt as to who was in charge. His hair was the color of Kansas dust, and his shirt was caked with sweat and dirt. When the riders reined in. nine rifles were out of their scabbards, aimed carelessly in John and Snyder's direction.

"Where ya think you're going, Johnny Reb?" the spokesman demanded contemptuously.

"To Caldwell," Snyder retorted. "Any law against that?"

"There's a law against bringing them tick-ridden critters behind you into this part of Kansas."

Snyder bristled. "Who's law?"

"*This* law!" He patted his rifle significantly.

John studied the riders intently. Two were obviously sod-busters. Their calloused hands spoke eloquently of long hours behind the plow, and they fingered their rifles uneasily. Three others, including the spokesman, were ranchers. They had the marks of the range upon them. But it was the remainder who concerned Breckenridge. They were dressed better than the rest, with tailor-made boots and fancy saddles and horses a cut better than those their companions rode. But it was their cold and emotionless eyes and the way they held their weapons that disturbed the young trail boss. They were hired guns, ready to kill at a nod from their employers.

"What if we go on?" asked Snyder.

"Then I reckon we'll have to stop you," the spokesman continued, his voice deceptively mild.

Snyder's lips quivered slightly. He wasn't used to being faced down. "And if ya don't?" he persisted. "What then?"

"There's twenty more of us in Caldwell and fifty in Wichita. If we don't stop you, they will. I ain't got no quarrel with you. Just turn that herd of yours west and there won't be no trouble."

A minute passed while Snyder and his Kansas adversary glared at each other.

"If we decide to come through to Abilene," Snyder snarled, "you'll be the first to know."

"We'll be waiting."

Snyder spat contemptuously and turned his big horse around. "Come on, John," he snarled. "Let's get where the company's better."

14

They rode south for half a mile without speaking.

"What do we do now?" the young trail boss asked.

"We've got to think on it. They don't have no right to do what they did. Kansas Governor Crawford signed a bill February 26, 1867, to protect Kansas livestock from Spanish Fever, as they call it. No Texas or Indian cattle was supposed to be drove into Kansas between March and December, except west of the sixth meridian and south of the settled parts."

"That include Abilene?" asked Breckenridge.

"Nope, but they decided to stretch the point a mite, seeing as how Abilene is on the railroad and all. They ain't enforced that bill since it was passed because the railroads and fellers a-making money off the herds put the pressure on. Now things is changing. The ranchers and settlers is taking things into their own hands. And the way I see it, the marshal's still a-going to look the other way, while them hired guns go to work." Snyder looked concerned.

"I know that," he continued, "but there's parts of that confounded bill they could use against us if they had a mind to. Before we bring our cattle into the state we're supposed to have them sold in Illinois or somewheres else, so's they won't stay in Kansas."

"That's what ya figgered on, ain't it?"

"They ain't sold yet. That's the problem. . . . If these Yanks is trying to stop us illegal, they'll try legal, too. And you can bet on it. When we get our cattle north of that border some two-bit sheriff or marshal's going to come along with a warrant for breaking the law. He'll ask to see my papers showing I've sold the herd east. If I ain't got it we'll be in a mess of trouble."

"So, what do we do?"

"I figger we'd best ride to Abilene, you and me. I know them buyers well. I'll get the herd sold and we'll go back and take our herd through, hired guns or no."

John thought he should go back to the herd, leaving Snyder alone on the trip to Abilene, but the boss insisted on the trail boss's company.

"The men can take care of the herd. I may need you in Abilene."

John shrugged. They were Snyder's cattle. If that was what he wanted it was all right with him. They turned their horses and rode north once more. They did not anticipate any problems, though they kept a close watch behind them for three hours. However, no one appeared. Apparently the Kansans thought their ultimatum to Snyder had caused him to lose his stomach for facing them.

They went into Caldwell for supplies and rode north across the Kansas prairie. The midsummer wind was at their backs, scorching the grass and drying the sweat on their shirts. The wind and heat combined with the harsh demands of the trail sapped their horses' strength and they stopped earlier than they planned to give the weary animals a rest. At their campsite there was a narrow stream, reduced to murky puddles of tepid, foul-tasting water. The grass, for as far as they could see, had been heavily grazed and pounded into the ground by ten thousand hooves.

"There ain't going to be much for our herd to eat when we get them up here," John said. "And there's still a long way to go."

"We'll have to move them fast and figger on losing weight," answered Snyder.

They cooked their bacon and beans over a small fire, finished the meal with a cup of coffee and crawled into their bedrolls. Shortly after daylight they were on their way again. They hadn't been riding long when they caught sight of a herd in the distance. At first they thought it was buffalo, but they knew that couldn't be; the buffalo had been driven west by the constant pressure of people.

"I didn't think there was a herd so close to us," Snyder said.

"There's a passel of cattle going north on the Chisholm this year," John replied. "Seems everybody wants to drive to Abilene."

They covered the next couple of miles in silence, lessening the distance between themselves and the Texas longhorns until they could see that the herd ahead was not moving.

"That's funny," Snyder muttered, "you'd think the trail boss'd have that herd on the way by this time of day."

As they drew near, the trail boss and one of his drovers rode back to meet them. When the stranger saw they were Texans he relaxed and returned his rifle to its scabbard. "I was afeared you was a couple of them Yankees trying to get us to move."

"We got a herd just below the line," Snyder explained. "Figgered we'd come up and get the lay of the land before we come on."

The trail boss cursed. "Wish we'd never heard of Abilene. That's what I wish."

"We drove up there last year," Snyder told him. "Figgered they did right good by us."

"We drove up there last year, too, and things worked out fine. For the herds as got here early, it worked out good. But now it's one big mess." He breathed deeply. "Would you believe it, there's cattle stacked all the way from here to Abilene and nobody knows how long it'll be till we get a chance to sell our herds. There ain't no railroad cars coming in to haul cattle east, and if there was, it wouldn't make no difference. *Nobody* in Abilene's buying these days."

Snyder rolled a cigarette and stuck it in his mouth, but held the match in his hand without lighting it. "I suppose it's that blasted fever them Yanks is so scared of."

The other Texan nodded. "I sure wouldn't bring no herd up here now, the way things is. I'm about to head west myself."

"As long as we've come this far I reckon me and Breckenridge will go on in to Abilene."

"Go ahead, if ya want to, but it won't do ya no good."

They stopped at the chuck wagon with him and had a cup of coffee before riding on. They passed the last of the cattle and rode another ten miles before they came upon another herd. The story there was the same as the first.

"The grass is about gone here," the rancher

informed Snyder. "If we don't get these critters sold soon we won't have any choice. We'll have to go west. The grass is giving out."

"Have you been to Abilene to see about selling them?"

"Just got back, but it didn't do no good. Them buyers is spooked for sure."

Snyder and John passed two more herds before reaching Abilene and heard tales of others off the trail who were trying to find enough grass to keep the cattle from losing weight. The rancher was glum and irritable that evening when they reached Abilene. They left their horses at the livery stable where John used to work, and got rooms at one of the nearby hotels. The next morning after breakfast, Snyder insisted they cross the tracks to one of the saloons.

"Most Texans go to the Bull's Head," John reminded him.

"Not this time," his boss snapped. "There ain't a better place in town than a saloon to find out what you want to know. So I'm going where the Yankees do their drinking. There'll be somebody setting around who knows everything that's a-going on and who's willing to spill it all for a beer."

When they went inside they were recognized as Texans by their hats and the dust on their clothes and were met with scowls from the other customers. There were two burly settlers at the far end of the bar and a handful of slim grim-faced cowhands and ranchers at three tables in the back. They glared at the newcomers. Even the bartender ignored the Texans as long as possible.

"Folks ain't very friendly around here," Snyder drawled.

"We're sort of particular about who we get friendly with," said a young hand who had had too much to drink.

Snyder's temper flared. "Just what do ya mean by that?"

"Make anything you want to make of it." The young man snarled as he pushed back from the table and staggered to his feet, his hand poised near the butt of his gun.

Snyder was more than willing to give him a fight, but Breckenridge turned his back on the cowhand deliberately and, taking Snyder's arm, guided him through the swinging doors into the cool morning air. The older man's jowls were livid.

"What'd you do that for?" he demanded.

"How long has it been since you fired that Colt you're wearing?"

Snyder hesitated. "Not so long."

"Have ya shot it in the last week?"

His companion shook his head.

"The last month?"

"I . . . I guess not."

"In the last three months?"

He took a deep breath. "I don't remember."

"If you even *think* you might face up to another man, you'd best be a-shooting most every day. Unless that guy's as rusty as you, he'd kill ya before your gun cleared the holster."

The rancher eyed him icily. "Where'd you learn that?"

John felt the color creep into his cheeks. "Never mind where I learned it. Just pay attention to what I say."

"There ain't no Yank a-going to insult me and get away with it. I've a mind to go back and call him."

"Now wait a minute!" John exclaimed. "Why'd you and me come all the way to Abilene, anyway? To take a chance of getting you killed, or finding out something about getting cattle into Kansas and on to Chicago?" They walked up the boardwalk together.

"There wasn't nobody in there who'd give us the time of day," the rancher said, changing the subject. "And I suppose that's the way it'll be everywhere."

"I got me an idea. Course it'll cost us something."

"I ain't going to bribe nobody."

"You don't have to. We can go over to the barbershop and have a haircut and a bath. That'll cost us 50¢ a piece. And another 15¢ for you if you get a shave."

"We ain't got time to fool around," Snyder retorted, "even if we do need to get cleaned up."

"You want to find out what's going on in Abilene, don't ya?" They went to the barbershop.

"Well, iffen it ain't Breckenridge!" the barber exclaimed when he saw him. "It's been a coon's age since I seen you. How're you doing?"

"Tolerable." He sat down on a chair near the window. "Thought we'd come in and get ourselves a bath and a haircut."

The barber nodded. "You know where the tub is. I'll get Gertie to fill it for you." The barber left them abruptly and went to the back where he called for his wife to fill the tub.

"You go first," John whispered. "I'll talk to him while you're having your bath."

There was little business in the shop that time of day and the barber sat down near him. "I see you didn't follow my advice about staying

167

away from them trail herds," he said as soon as Snyder left the room. "Now you've bought yourself a heap of trouble."

"I understand the ranchers and settlers have got together."

"And they've brought in some guns from the outside."

"I've heard that, too."

"Only the trouble ought to be about over now. Though what's going to happen to all them longhorns waiting around town has got me."

"What's happened to change everything?"

"We got word that the Illinois legislature passed a bill keeping Texas cattle from the tick belt out of the state, so they can't sell to Chicago. There ain't no market!"

John stared at him. That would account for the cattle backed up around Abilene. "You're sure of that?"

"As sure as I'm a-setting here. If you want to read more about it, go over to the newspaper office and ask to see the issue that's got the story. The herds that got up here after the bill passed had to be sold for their hides."

Young Breckenridge's head whirled, but he managed to control his facial expression. "That's right interesting."

"Yeah. That boss of yours might not even be able to pay you. I warned ya to stay away from them Texas herds, but you wouldn't listen!"

15

Snyder was dismayed by the news John picked up in the barbershop, but he was unwilling to accept it as truth. He insisted on going to the newspaper office.

The barber hadn't exaggerated. There it was in bold headline type: Illinois Nixes Texas Cattle."

Snyder paid for the paper and they went out on the boardwalk. There was no doubt about it; a law had been made against cattle from the tick area of Texas entering Illinois. It wasn't the way it ought to be, the rancher reasoned. Anybody from Texas knew that the cattle in the big herds were as healthy as any. But the law was the law.

"I guess that does it," John said. He couldn't help feeling sorry for Snyder. Practically everything the rancher had was tied up in that herd; now he was trapped with them. He couldn't even give them away for shipment to Chicago.

They were still standing on the boardwalk when a slight, dapper little man in a neat black suit and bowler hat came up to them. He was swarthy, almost as dark as the native Sioux. His black hair was slicked down in a futile effort to control the curls, and a neat moustache and sideburns gave him a sophistication uncommon on the streets of Abilene. John noticed he had followed them into the newspaper office and had been listening to their conversation. Now he wanted to talk.

"Let me guess: You've got a herd out there that you was a-fixing to sell for shipping to Chicago. Now you can't do it."

Snyder stared contemptuously at him. "What's it to you?"

The well-dressed stranger sidled closer. "I know how it is." He lowered his voice. "I'm a Johnny Reb myself. Name's Louis LeFleur. Come up from New Orleans three years ago after fighting the war with General Lee. I'm going to let you in on a little secret. There's a way around that law. All you have to do is have the right connections."

"Meaning what?" Snyder asked, interested.

"You don't think all those cattle being held around Abilene are going to be butchered for their hides, do you?"

"I couldn't rightly say it makes a lot of difference to me one way or the other."

LeFleur glanced about stealthily. "Let's go over to the Bull's Head where we can find a quiet corner and talk."

They followed him to the saloon frequented by the Texas ranchers and their drovers. Snyder led the way to the far corner where he signaled for the bartender to send over a bottle of whiskey. The waiter brought the bottle and three glasses. John pushed his away. His companions eyed him questioningly but acted as though they had seen nothing unusual in his action.

"Now," LeFleur began in a coarse whisper, "it's this way. The government left a hole as big as a chuck wagon in that law. You can get yourself a swear paper saying your herd has been wintered out of the tick area. You not only can get them into Kansas without any trouble, you can take them on to Kansas City and ship them to Chicago where you'll get top prices—better than what they've been paying before this tick thing started causing trouble."

"It'll never work," Snyder said aloud. "Most of my herd's covered with ticks. They'd take one look and know they'd never wintered no place outside of Texas."

The stanger's smile informed him that he had already considered that possibility and had worked it out. "You forget who you're dealing with. I got us a place where we can get your herd across the border without any trouble at all. And I've got a friend close to Kansas City who'll hold them until cold weather. The first hard freeze'll take care of the ticks and you'll be on your way." He paused in confidence. "That's what most of those owners with herds waiting around Abilene are fixing to do. It's going to cost them, but they'll make out real good. And so can you."

Snyder pulled in a deep breath and the corners of his moustache twitched. "I don't know you, LeFleur, but I'm a cattleman, not a crook! Before I'd do what you're saying I'd see the whole kaboodle of my herd dead." His voice raised. "Now, get outta my sight!"

LeFleur shrank from Snyder's anger. "Be stubborn, for all I care, but I'm warning you. I've got the only way of getting your herd to the eastern market and you know it!"

Snyder downed the last of his glass of whiskey and turned to John. "We're wasting our time."

They went to their horses in silence and rode out of Abilene.

"You know," Snyder said at last, "I wonder if maybe he didn't have something, after all."

"Maybe we could hold them up here for the winter and ship to Chicago come spring," Breckenridge said. "That way we could get a swear paper legal-like."

"You've got a point. But where can we find grass enough for a herd the size of ours for all winter?" He rode on for several minutes without speaking. "And if we did find the grass, what about water? It ain't easy to find both in these parts. Especially with so many cattle around here right now."

"We've got to do something."

"The onliest thing I can think of is to head west and north till we find a rancher wanting to build up his herd or an army post as needs meat. It'll take some doing, but we'll get rid of our herd legal-like. We won't pull no tricks with phony papers."

They rode back to where the drovers were holding the herd and turned them west to the trail that led through Dodge City to Ogallala in the new state of Nebraska. Some of the hands grumbled when they learned of the change in plans. They wanted to push north to Abilene in spite of the opposition. Most had fought in the war between the states and were spoiling for a fight. They would have looked upon winning a skirmish with the Kansans as a form of vindication for losing the war.

But common sense told them it was not wise to add their herd to the others that were waiting impatiently at Abilene. Even if they got past the

172

opposing force they would be stopped short of the railroad, and that would not be good. In the end they went along without complaint.

It made for a much longer drive, but the longhorns were as tough as the men who pushed them over the rough terrain, and they were tireless on the trail. They seemed to have an inner reserve of stamina that was not apparent in any other breed, save the buffalo that were born to the harsh climate and sparse grass. When they reached a stretch without water holes, which often happened, they could go for two days with nothing to drink. They seemed to possess a sixth sense when it came to locating water. Let them get a sniff of water, miles away, and they would take off, heads high and strides lengthening.

When that happened, experienced hands usually let them go. They knew how difficult it would be to turn the herd when the sweet smell of that life-sustaining element was in their nostrils. Only if the drovers chanced to be aware that the water was tainted with alkali or some natural poison would they risk their necks to change the course of the lead cow and move the herd in another direction.

The herd was stubborn and difficult. Critters that hadn't given trouble for weeks were suddenly as obstinate and cunning as mountain lions in their efforts to escape the watchful eyes of the drovers. A longhorn would be moving with the herd, docile and uncomplaining as a milk cow, when he would whirl without warning and dash away. Then, as though on cue, a dozen more would thunder after him. On those occasions, the stiletto-sharp horns were particularly dangerous. Most of the drovers had seen friends or associates gored or mangled in such a melee.

But for all the problems involved in trailing longhorns, John and his drovers made comparatively good time on their way west. They were north of the mesquite and greasewood, but sage and cacti and Spanish sword dotted the prairie, thinning the grass. The cattle became even more lean and scrawny than before, but there was no evidence by the way they stepped out to indicate they were weakening because of limited grazing. They were accustomed to scrounging for feed.

At last they reached Ogallala, Nebraska, just north of the Platte River. Snyder had been talking about the possibility of going all the way to Montana, but that was a long haul. John wanted to go on without stopping at the wild little frontier town but Snyder insisted.

"Them riders who were with us for supper last night was a-saying there's a cattle buyer for the army in town," the rancher said. "If we can sell the herd and give delivery here, we'll save ourselves a heap of riding."

"Maybe so, but the weather's good now and we ought to take advantage of it," Breckenridge said. "We're already well into August and we've got a long haul to Montana. The snow's going to be dusting the trail before we get there, iffen we don't stay with it."

"It won't take all that long to talk with one buyer," Snyder insisted. So they bedded down the herd a few miles out of town and the rancher rode off to Ogallala in an effort to locate the army agent. He had been gone half a day when the Ogallala marshal rode out to see him. The marshal located John and asked for Josiah Snyder.

"He's in town," young Breckenridge said.

"Wish I'd knowed it. I could've saved myself a ride."

"Is there something wrong?"

The marshal cleared his throat. "He ain't in no trouble with the law," he answered, "but there is something wrong at home, according to a feller by the name of Mike Wahl."

"He'd be the foreman. He was supposed to be the trail boss on this drive before he got stabbed in a bunkhouse ruckus."

"I figgered he was something like that."

"It's Belle, ain't it?" John asked, knowing even before he asked what the answer would be.

"She died a month or more ago. Guess they been having some trouble finding you." The marshal gathered up his mount's reins. "I'd just as well head for town. . . . Any chance of you a-going with me?"

"Reckon so."

Breckenridge left the herd in charge of Bruce Todd, one of the older, more stable drovers, then he and the marshal set out for Ogallala. They found Josiah Snyder in one of the saloons, sitting alone at a table, a bottle in front of him.

He looked up as he saw John and the marshal approaching. "Don't tell me you're the buyer I rode all the way to town to see."

The stranger pulled out a chair and sat across from the Texas rancher. "I'm the marshal."

Snyder's eyes met his. "Everything else has gone wrong on this drive. I suppose I should've expected something like this. . . ." He sighed, resigned to the inevitable. "What've we done to bring the law on us?"

"Nothing at all." He fished a note from his shirt pocket. "I've got a message for you that came by way of Abilene and Dodge. They said you was a-heading this way. . . . I've been a-looking for you for the last week or so."

"What is it?" For the first time the anger left Snyder's voice.

"It come from a feller by the name of Wahl."

"My foreman." The rancher's hand was trembling as he took the envelope, ripped it open, and read the message inside. The color fled from his cheeks, leaving them blanched and gray. John's heart ached for Snyder as the older man stared at the note.

"It ... It's Belle," he whispered hoarsely. "She's gone!"

"I know," John said softly.

Snyder snapped erect, black eyes blazing. "You *knew?*" he cried, unmindful of the others around them. "How'd you know? Answer me that!"

"Before we left she ... she told me she was feeling so poorly she couldn't make the trip this time." He saw the rage building in Snyder's features. He knew what was coming and he didn't blame him. But he had to tell Snyder the truth. He couldn't keep it bottled inside any longer. "I think she was afeared this would happen. I know I was."

The rancher grasped the table with both hands and tightened his grip until the veins stood out. "Why didn't you tell me?" he demanded.

"She made me promise not to. Made me give my word I wouldn't say nothing to nobody."

Silence gripped the usually noisy saloon. Even the bartender stopped what he was doing, stunned by the scene before him.

"She was my wife," he continued. "I had a right to know."

Pain twisted John's youthful face. "If it had been up to me I'd have told you right off! Don't you see? She made me promise!"

For a time it was as though Snyder were all alone. His grip relaxed and he sprawled in his chair, the strength draining from his powerful frame.

"If I'd knowed about it," he muttered helplessly, "I could've stayed home. Maybe there was something I could've done for her. Something to . . . to have stopped this from happening."

John wanted to speak, to protest that there was nothing anyone could have done, but Snyder would not have heard him. He was like one in a trance.

Finally the big man stirred, wrenched himself upright, and reached for the bottle in front of him. Tilting it, he pulled in a long, deep draught. Then slamming it noisily on the table, he wiped his mouth with the back of his hand and glared balefully at John.

Hesitating, young Breckenridge asked, "D-don't ya think we ought to go now?"

"Go?" Snyder bellowed. "Where would I go?"

"Back to the herd. The men are a-going to be wondering what happened to us."

At first he thought Snyder was going to go with him. Grasping the table for support, the distraught man started to stand. Half out of the chair, however, he changed his mind and settled back. "I ought to kill you for what you done!" he snarled.

"I don't blame you and I'm sorry."

"Sorry?" He was shouting now. "Sorry? A lot of good that'll do!" He took another drink, bigger than the first. "Get outta here! *Get outta my sight!* I never want to see you again!"

For a time John sat there helplessly, but the marshal motioned him to leave. "Stay out of his way for a bit," he said, so softly he didn't think the rancher heard him. "He'll feel different once he's had some time to think about it."

"You're right about one thing, marshal!" Snyder cried. "I will feel different. Next time I'll probably put a bullet through his gizzard!"

John Breckenridge got up and left. For a time he remained on the boardwalk in front of the Front Street Saloon. By then, night had settled on the grubby little town. The general store and the bank and the blacksmith shop were closed. In fact, only the saloons and the hotel were open. He didn't want to leave Snyder—especially at a time like this. But he had no choice. If he remained, the rancher might draw on him, and he sure didn't want that kind of trouble on top of what they had already.

16

Because he didn't know what else to do, John finally got his horse and rode out to where the drovers were holding the herd. Those men who had ridden for the Walking S in other years and had known Belle were almost as disturbed as John was by her death.

"She was a good woman," one of the older hands said. "Sorta kept Josiah on the straight and narrow."

Another grizzled drover nodded. "Makes me wonder what'll happen to him now that he won't have her around to ride herd on him."

The original plan had been to start moving north again the following morning if Snyder hadn't been able to find the buyer for the army and make a deal. But John had to hold the herd where it was since Snyder hadn't come back and they couldn't go on without him.

"I think you'd best ride into town again and see if you can find that army guy," Todd said. "We've got to do something about this herd, pronto."

"That's not a bad idea." John breathed deeply. "I'll try to get hold of Snyder and get him back here."

"I wouldn't want that job. He's a wild cat when he's drunk!"

Breckenridge saddled the big sorrel and started over the low, rolling hills towards Ogallala. He was dreading another confrontation with Snyder. He didn't want to have trouble with one who meant so much to him. It was sort of like fighting with Ma when she was alive, or Waddy Ross.

John wasn't quite prepared for what he had to do when he crested the tallest hill on the trail into town and saw the squalid cluster of crumbling, unpainted clapboard buildings below him. The general store looked so much like the one in Weaverville, with its broken-down porch and faded sign, that he could almost see Roy Ingerton on the porch, a dirty apron fastened about his big belly.

There was no need to look any farther than Front Street for Josiah Snyder. His horse was still tied to the hitching rail in front of the saloon, where it probably had been all night. John reined in and dismounted, tethering Rusty beside the rancher's blue-roan. Out of habit his fingers checked his gun as unobtrusively as possible, and he started for the saloon.

The same bartender was on duty, serving a dusty young cowhand a beer. He recognized John immediately and came over to him. "Your man's still here," he said in low tones. "Come in this morning soon as we opened. Ain't hardly moved outta that chair since."

"I'll go over and talk to him."

"Don't think it'll do you no good. He's really tying one on."

"You know why, don't you?"

The bartender nodded.

John went over to Snyder, who was sprawled

in his chair in a drunken stupor. He spoke sharply to him, but the rancher didn't respond. While Breckenridge stood there, Josiah moved slightly and opened his eyes once. John thought the drunken man recognized him but his eyes closed almost immediately and the trail boss could not be sure.

"I tell you it ain't doing no good," the bartender told him. "He's out of it. He wouldn't know what you was a-saying, even if he was awake."

"I'll come back in a few hours."

"You do that. . . . And I'll try to get him to ease off and maybe eat something."

John took Snyder's horse to the livery barn, paid the hostler for his keep for the day, and directed him to take good care of the barrel-chested steed. Once that was accomplished he went over to the café, got himself some coffee, and waited.

However, that was useless. When John went back to the saloon Snyder was awake, but he was sullen and uncooperative.

"I told you I never wanted to see you again!" he slurred.

John ignored the rancher's bitter anger. "We've got a herd waiting. Let's get something to eat and go back so's we can get them moving."

Snyder straightened and pointed toward his trail boss. "*You* ain't got no cattle to move. *I've* got a herd out there. . . . But you don't work for the Walking S no more! I fired you!"

"Come on, Snyder. Put that bottle down, pay your bill, and let's go have something to eat."

The rancher pushed him away clumsily with a swing of his arm. "I ain't going nowheres. I'm a-staying here with my friends." He wrapped his fingers around the bottle. Tears came to his eyes. "I've got nowheres to go. Belle's dead. . . . Did you hear that? She's dead!"

"I know, Josiah, and I'm terrible sorry, but it don't do no good to sit here and drink. We've got to get them cattle up to Montana and time's a-running out." He laid a hand on the rancher's shoulder. "That herd's got to start a-moving. Every day we lose is a-going to cause us trouble finishing the drive before winter hits."

Snyder took another drink. "Go on! Get outta here before I take a shot at ya. . . . That's what I oughta do!"

Reluctantly, John turned and stalked toward the door, his spurs jangling raucously on the floor. There was no use trying to talk to Snyder when he was in this shape.

"I'm going over to the hotel and get a room," he told the bartender. "I've got to be here to get hold of him when he's ready to sober up. Send someone to get me when you think he'll listen." John took Rusty to the stable. "I may be around for awhile," he told the hostler. "But until I leave I want you to take good care of him."

For several days young Breckenridge remained in Ogallala. He checked on his boss three times, but there was little change. Where Snyder went when the saloon was closed no one seemed to know. Perhaps to the hotel or the boarding-house. Perhaps to the livery barn loft. But wherever it was, he must have taken a bottle along—he was always drunk in the morning.

The third morning, Snyder didn't go to the saloon immediately, but started for the café in the hotel. He staggered along the boardwalk, a bottle in each hand. Half the distance to his destination he stopped and vomited in the gutter. A woman walking by wrinkled her nose and got as far from him as possible. As soon as he was able to move again he turned and wobbled back to the saloon where he took his place at the same table. He was there when John came to check on him later, self-pity bringing tears to his eyes.

John tried to talk to him then, but only succeeded in causing the tears to flow more freely.

"You can talk," he muttered. "You ain't been married, so you don't know what it's like to lose your wife. Nobody knows!"

"Stop that bawling, Josiah, and quit drinking this-a-way. You've got to sober up!"

"You leave me alone." He jerked himself free from the hand John had laid on his shoulder. "You can't tell me what to do!"

Young Breckenridge left presently. He could have the bartender quit selling Snyder whiskey but that would be useless. He'd only bluster around and maybe get himself or someone else in bad trouble. Besides, there were plenty of other saloons in Ogallala. He would move to one of them.

John and the rancher had been in town almost a week without any indication of how much longer it would be until Snyder got himself straightened out when Todd, the drover John had left in charge, rode in.

"We had a drifter stop by last night who plumb scared me," he said. "He just came in from Bozeman and was a-telling us that they'd had a sprinkling of snow ten days ago. Word's out that it looks like Montana's due for an early winter."

"I been trying to tell Snyder we've got to get moving, but he don't seem to hear me."

"That ain't all our problems. Them fifteen-hundred-odd head take a sight of grass to keep their bellies full and right now the land we're pasturing is a-getting mighty thin. We're going to have to move them critters in a day or two and I don't know where to go to find as much grass as we need."

John sighed. "I'll go to the saloon again, but don't count on me being able to do much."

"Want I should go along?"

Breckenridge thought about that. "I'd best talk to him alone. I don't know how he'd take it if he saw you and me together. Might get the idea we're ganging up on him. He can be right stubborn if he's a mind to. Especially when he's like he is now."

Young Breckenridge left the café and hurried up the street to the saloon. Snyder was still there, head and arms resting on the table. He was sleeping, and it was impossible to waken him.

"Has he been like that all day?" John asked the bartender.

"He sleeps awhile, then he wakes up and drinks and cries awhile."

"Think I'll stick around till he wakes up again."

"I'll quit selling to him if you say so."

John shrugged. "He'd as well be drinking here as up the street. Besides, the shape he's in, he might cause trouble if you stop. . . . I'll have to figger some other way of getting him sober."

He went over and was about to sit at a small table when a grizzled old mountain man sidled up, eyeing him momentarily. After a time the younger man became aware of his presence.

"Something bothering you?" John asked quietly.

"Yes sir." The old man's voice was shrill and

loud, carrying to the far corners of the room. "Yes sirree, there's something a-bothering me. You're the spitting image of a friend of mine. Ain't seen him for years, but he was the fastest man with a gun I ever seen."

John squirmed uncomfortably. His questioner hobbled closer, squinting at him with watery eyes.

"Ever hear of a gunman by the name of George Breckenridge?"

John pretended not to understand.

"Yes sirree, Bob!" the man went on, "you sure do look like George! . . ." He turned and raised his voice even though that was not necessary to make everyone in the room aware of what he was saying. "Let me tell you something! This here young feller looks exactly like George Breckenridge.

"If you never heard of Breckenridge, he was a man! Him and me and another gunfighter by the name of Waddy Ross used to work together. But neither me or Waddy could hold a candle to our friend George. One time I seen him take on three hired guns, cool as a cucumber." He paused, defying anyone to doubt his word. "And when the smoke all cleared, he'd laid them out like so many sticks of timber, all in a row." With that he turned back to John. "Sure you don't know Breckenridge?"

The trail boss frowned. It wasn't wise to answer the old man straight out. He ought to pass it off or lie to him; that was the only safe way for him to handle the matter—the only way he could be sure of avoiding a showdown with someone who thought he might be faster with a gun. But he was so upset by his failure to get Snyder sober that his mind wasn't nimble enough to avoid the old man's questions. And lying wasn't in him, so he told the truth.

"I reckon I knew George Breckenridge," he said, pride honing his voice. "I ought to. He was my pa."

"I knowed it!" the old man chortled. "I knowed the first time I seed you." He directed his attention to his audience. "Didn't I tell ya this young feller was the spitting image of my friend, George?" He turned to John once more. "My name's Gabe Gillette. And I'm right proud to shake your hand! . . . Now, would you do me the honor of letting me buy you a drink?"

"No, thanks." Breckenridge smiled to soften the refusal. He thought that would disturb the old man but it didn't.

"I shoulda remembered. That pa of yourn wasn't much for the hard stuff, neither. Now, Waddy Ross, him and me'd take a nip now and again, but your pa wanted to keep his eye sharp and his hand quick. I shoulda knowed you wouldn't be having any."

Embarrassed at the sudden hush that settled over the saloon and the awe in the stares of some of the men, he went out quickly. He paused in front of the saloon. He still hadn't accomplished his purpose of getting Snyder sober, but it would be best to wait for an hour or two until most of the men who were now in the saloon had drifted on. Situations like this could be dangerous. Word of his identity would spread, and some wild-eyed cowhand or drifter might get the idea of building a reputation for himself in a hurry.

He went back to the hotel café where Todd was waiting. "Get the herd and the men ready to move," he said. "I'll be along with Snyder if I have to hog-tie him and throw him across his saddle like a sack of beans."

"That's the best news I've heard since we stopped here."

When Todd was gone John went inside and ordered a cup of coffee and a couple of doughnuts. Before he finished, two men who had been in the saloon earlier came to talk to him. They wanted to know more about his pa and some of the gunfights he had been in. They asked how many men he had killed and what he had taught John about handling a gun. They wouldn't believe him when he said his pa hadn't taught him anything about using a handgun and left muttering angrily. When they finally went back outside, he paid for his lunch and made his way to the saloon.

The old man was still there, waiting. "I knowed you'd be back. There are some things I've got to talk to you about."

John wished he would go away, but his new, self-appointed friend was not ready for that. He pulled out a chair and sat down.

"Let me tell you about the time me and Waddy and that pa of yourn cleaned out the nestors as was crowding the spread we was a-working for. You shoulda seen us!" His high, cackling laughter echoed above the clatter of the piano that had just started to play.

John only half listened. And when the old man finally stopped talking, he got to his feet. "Sorry, old timer," he said, "but I've got to check on my friend."

He was a table or two away from Snyder when a youngster of sixteen or so jumped in front of him, legs spraddled and his hand poised tautly over his gun. The crowd in the saloon melted silently to one side or the other, endeavoring to get out of the line of fire. Only Snyder remained seated as his mind was too befuddled to grasp what was about to take place.

"Where do you think you're going?" the boy demanded, shouting to be heard above the tinny sound of the player piano.

It was obvious to John that liquor was speaking. The young stranger's face was flushed and his words slurred.

"Over to help my friend," Breckenridge said. He spoke carefully. It was one of those tense moments when the wrong word or move could cause an explosion. "Stand aside."

"Not for the likes of you, I ain't moving! You ain't no son of George Breckenridge. You're a liar!"

"Them are strong words. Now, step aside."

A snear twisted his adversary's face. "Why don't you make me?"

"I ain't got no quarrel with you."

"Let's see how fast this son of George Breckenridge really is!"

John took a step forward, his left hand clenched, his right hovering near the handle of his six-gun. His mouth was dry and coppery and his lips trembled. Fear licked at his resolve, but he shoved it aside. He had heard men boast that they had never known the bitter taste of fear, but Waddy told him such braggarts had never faced a gun about to be fired in anger; and Waddy was one who knew what he was talking about.

He was afraid, but the man he faced wouldn't know it. "Don't push me! Move aside."

For an instant the boy wavered and it would

have been over without bloodshed, except that a cowhand spoke suddenly. Involuntarily young Breckenridge glanced in the direction of the voice. The sallow youth who faced him thought he saw an advantage, the extra split second he needed to get his Colt clear of the holster and fire.

John recovered quickly and spun back to face the boy, but not quickly enough. He saw the wild-eyed youth jerk his iron from its holster. Instinctively, he acted. Whipping out his own weapon and diving to one side, he squeezed the trigger. Just then, hot lead burned a hole into his hip just above the bone, and his frame wrenched convulsively. For the first time in his life he felt the searing blow of a .45 slug.

In that instant he saw a spot of red stain on his assailant's shirt just above the belt spread slowly. Surprise gleamed suddenly in the young boy's eyes, as though he could not believe what had happened. For an instant he stared at John, and his lips parted as though he was about to speak. Then his knees sagged, and he crumpled to the floor. Men rushed to the boy as blood gushed from the wound, staining the floor. He groaned in pain and lay still.

"Somebody get the doc," the bartender cried.

"Ain't no use in that now," old Gabe observed. "There's nothing no doc can do for him."

That was all that John heard. He felt the numbness spread from his hip down into his leg and up to his rib cage. At first there was no pain, only the realization that he had been shot. He closed his eyes and fought the nausea that swept over him. That was the last he knew.

17

Snyder stared stupidly at John, who was lying motionless on the saloon floor. Grasping the table with both hands, he struggled to get to his feet, but the effort failed. He settled back into the battered chair, his eyes slitted as he fought to breathe. John opened his eyes and stirred uneasily. Someone he had never seen before knelt beside him.

"He was just fighting a kid!" someone beyond the circle of his vision said angrily.

"But the other guy started it and drew first," the bartender put in. "We *all* know that!"

Murmurs of assent came from around the room, agreeing with the one behind the bar that the youth who had been killed had provoked the fight by drawing his weapon first.

"I still don't think the kid shoulda been killed. He was so young he didn't know what he was a-doing. That Johnny Reb oughta have winged him."

"Winged him?" Old Gillete exclaimed. "Iffen he'd tried that, he'd have been the one to die!"

The bartender nodded grimly. "You know who that kid is, don't ya?"

The stranger shook his head. "All I know is I got a boy as old as that at home and he ain't no match for no gunman. If he was the one a-lying there, I'd be a-hanging me somebody!"

"That *kid* you're a-feeling sorry for is Aaron Shreves. Like you said, he was only a snot-nosed kid, but when he strapped on that gun he figgered he was big as anybody. . . . Over at Silver City in Colorado Territory he killed four men. And he wasn't too particular about giving them a chance, either. They tell me he was as sweet and innocent as a sidewinder."

By that time the one who had bent over John looked up. "Two of you give me a hand," he ordered crisply. "I've got to get him over to my office where I can work on him."

Snyder heard that and managed to stand erect. "You ain't taking him nowheres. He's my trail boss. We've got to get him to a doc!"

"If you wasn't so drunk, you'd see that I *am* a doctor!"

"Well, iffen you're a doc, don't just stand there. Do something!"

The gaunt, angular man by John's side, who looked more like a gambler than a doctor, glared at Snyder and turned deliberately. "All right boys," he said, "let's get him over to the office. I've got to stop that bleeding and take out that slug."

Snyder reached for the bottle but stopped with it halfway to his lips and slammed it on the table. "I'm going along!" he announced to no one in particular. He staggered a few steps on his way to the swinging doors, but by the time he crossed the street and followed the strange procession up the block to the doctor's office, few would even have noticed he had been drinking.

The doctor looked up as he came in. "If you stay here you've got to keep out of the way and be quiet."

Snyder ignored him. "You've got to save him!" he stammered desperately. "He's all I got left, now that Belle's dead!"

Grimly the doctor set to work. He removed John's cowhide chaps and cut away his jeans and underwear to expose the ugly wound. Then he gave him a stiff dose of laudanum and an injection of hyoscine, morphine, and cactine. By the time he had his surgical instruments ready, the pain was deadened by the medication. He dug out the slug using a pair of long-nosed forceps. Then he began to clean out the wound, removing pieces of leather from the chaps, and cloth from the underwear and jeans. The only antiseptic he had was whiskey, and he used it liberally. Working with care, he finished the task and sewed up the wound.

By this time Josiah Snyder was sober, though he still had the stench of whiskey about him, and his face was flushed and puffy.

"Doc," he managed, "is . . . is he going to be all right?"

The doctor did not reply until he finished washing the last of the blood from his hands and wiped them on a grimy towel hanging over the basin.

"That slug didn't hit any arteries or vital organs. And he's healthy as one of them longhorn bulls you're herding. If he don't get an infection I reckon he's got a good chance."

John Breckenridge knew nothing of what was going on. He woke up once or twice during the night and stirred restlessly, not realizing where he was or what had happened. He sensed only the terrible pain in his hip that radiated up and down his entire left side. The instant he moved, both the doctor and Snyder were with him.

The next morning the doctor sent Snyder to the hotel for some chicken broth. John protested that he wasn't hungry, but they made him eat it. When he once more drifted off into a fitful, uneasy sleep, the rancher talked with the doctor about finding a place for his young trail boss to stay where someone would take care of him. "We've got to get that herd to moving as soon as we can," he said, "but I ain't a-going nowheres till we find somebody to take good care of him."

"There's the boardinghouse," Doc said, "but I don't know as Amy'd be the best to take care of your man. . . . If they'll do it, Matt Norvall and his wife over at the hotel would be my pick. They run a good place and do what they say they will." He nodded for emphasis. "If I was in your place that's where I'd go. They could put him in one of the back rooms where it'd be nice and quiet, and his missus would take care of him real good. . . ."

Snyder left the doctor's office abruptly, went to the hotel, and made arrangements for the Norvalls to take care of John. He paid what they thought was adequate, and made arrangements to take care of anything extra when he came back through on the way to Texas.

For several days John was scarcely aware that he had been moved. He remembered the pain of being jostled as they lifted him in the doctor's office and carried him along the boardwalk to the hotel. He remembered the cool breeze of the morning and the sounds of wagons rattling over the rough, dusty street. And he felt the clean, newly washed sheets when he was finally settled in bed in a room next to the Norvall family quarters in the Princess Hotel. But the days ran together until he didn't know one from the other.

At first the doctor came over twice a day concerned about his fever and periods of delirium. He drained the pus from the wound, doused it liberally with whiskey, and wrapped it again. After each visit Rebecca Norvall wrinkled her nose distastefully every time she came into the room.

"Smells like a saloon," she grumbled. "I'll be glad when he can start using regular medicine."

Sometimes John heard her and sometimes he didn't when periods of hallucination were upon him. After a week or so his temperature began to drop and the delirium lessened. Then the doctor came by only once a day and finally was able to discontinue the application of whiskey to the wound. That was much to Rebecca's satisfaction since now she could allow her daughters to bring in his meals when she was busy.

Elizabeth, who was seventeen and a more attractive edition of her severe-featured mother, came sweeping in with his meal, set it on the stand beside the bed and went out. She spoke to him and answered his questions, but that was all. Helen, however, came to see John whenever she got a chance. She was a vivacious thirteen-year-old; a long-legged tomboy with a reddish glint to her hair and freckles across the bridge of her nose. She preferred climbing trees and riding horses to playing dolls.

"You know why Elizabeth don't stay and talk, don't you?" she asked on one occasion, sitting across from him, keeping him company while he ate.

"Hadn't thought much about it."

"It's that night clerk, Charlie Sims. She's sweet on him. Says he's the handsomest man she ever saw."

John drank his coffee without speaking.

"Charlie's sweet on Elizabeth, too," she chattered, "but he's jealous. Every time he comes to see her he asks if she's been visiting you again. Pa says he's afeared they're a-going to want to get married one of these days. He don't like Charlie much. Says he's lazy and too pretty to be a real man. But Ma sticks up for Elizabeth. She thinks Charlie would be wonderful for her."

"How about you?" John asked, amused by her appraisal of the situation.

"Me?" She wrinkled her nose distastefully. "He wears spats!" she said, as though that was all the explanation necessary to reveal her attitude toward Charlie Sims.

"You know," John said one day when homesickness was sweeping over him, "I've got a sister a little younger than you."

Her eyes brightened. "Where does she live?"

"Up in Wyoming Territory," he told her. "My step-pa has a ranch out of Weaverville."

She didn't know where that was, but it didn't matter. She wanted to know all about Miriam. Did she like to ride horseback? Did her ma make her help clean the house and do the dishes?

"I hate things like that," she explained.

"I'm afeared Miriam gets in on a lot of work around the house," he said. "Our ma's dead and she has to take care of Fletch and our step-pa. There ain't no one else to do it."

Tears filled her eyes. "Oh, that's too bad. . . . About your ma, I mean. You must miss her an awful lot."

After that they became very good friends. Helen brought her pa's checkers and dominoes in, and they played endlessly.

"Ma doesn't like it when we play dominoes," she told him. "The Chinese use them for gambling and I guess she's scared Elizabeth and me'll get the habit. But Pa says lots and lots of people play dominoes without ever betting, so Ma says we can."

Three weeks after the shooting, John was able to get up and dress. Using a cane which Matt brought helped to ease the boredom.

Actually, though, it was Helen who made the hours pass swiftly. She tired of playing games after a few days, but found some books in her pa's library and started reading to him.

"This one's Pa's favorite," she said. "It doesn't have too many big words. Would you like to have me read it to you?" She waited hopefully for his answer.

"Well now," he said. "I reckon that'd be just great." He picked the book up and looked at it. *"Robinson Crusoe.* Can't say I ever seen this one before."

"Oh, it's good. It's so sad it'll make you cry. . . . You *like* to cry when you read a book, don't you?"

"Can't say as I ever cried reading a book," he said. When he saw the disappointment in her eyes, he added, "Of course I've been knocking around and ain't had no chance to read much."

That seemed to satisfy her. She opened the book and began to read aloud to him. She read surprisingly well for her age. John could tell that either her pa or ma had spent a lot of time helping her.

Being with Helen made him even more homesick than before. He wondered if Miriam looked like Ma now and how much she had grown. She ought to be quite a young lady by this time. He hoped she would be as nice as the younger Norvall girl. He was sure she was. She would have to be, having a ma like theirs.

As time passed, especially when Helen started school that fall, John grew increasingly restless. He wished Snyder hadn't left a note telling him to wait in Ogallala till he and Todd got back. It would have been good to go up to Weaverville and see Miriam and his stepfather. He even missed Fletch. In spite of the trouble between them, he cared for his stepbrother. They had grown up on the same ranch and had lived in the same house for six years.

John went out for walks every morning as soon as he was able, trying to strengthen his hip. At first he could only manage a block or so but as the days passed, he grew stronger till he could walk as much and as fast as before. He always went as far as the stable to curry his big sorrel. And, when he felt strong enough to ride, he saddled Rusty and took him out.

John still had plenty of time on his hands and tried to busy himself around the hotel. He helped Matt repair the back step and put new glass in a couple of windows. He shingled the barn and re-hung several doors so they would close and latch properly. In spite of the work he found to occupy himself, there was still too much time for him to sit around and think.

Weeks had passed since the shooting when Snyder had sobered up and moved out with the herd. John was beginning to wonder if something had happened to keep them from reaching Montana. Maybe Snyder had gone into one of the few towns along the trail and started drinking again. That wasn't like him, but it hadn't been like him to drink for so long after he got word that Belle had died, either. But that day in Ogallala when he heard of Belle's death, he seemed to have gone out of his mind. If it hadn't been for the gunfight and John's getting shot he didn't know how long Snyder might have stayed drunk.

Gabe Gillette, the old mountain man, came to the hotel twice to visit with John, spinning long, rambling tales of the times he had ridden with Waddy Ross and George Breckenridge. But on the third visit he didn't come to talk about the old days.

"Could we go to your room?" he asked mysteriously. "I'd sorta like to talk to you private."

John glanced about the spacious lobby. It was midday and the clerk was the only other person in the room, save Helen, who had been reading to him.

"We can talk here."

Gabe shook his head. "Nope. Not for what I've got to say."

John led him to his room and closed the door behind them. Even then Gabe Gillette scooted his chair close to John's and lowered his hoarse voice to a whisper.

"Everyone thinks I'm just a mountain man, interested in trapping and buying fur these past years since I quit riding with your pa and Waddy, but that ain't true. I been prospecting up in Montana Territory. I got me a snug little cabin and the sweetest gold mine you ever did see."

John's eyes widened in surprise.

"Yes sirree, Bob." He allowed himself a thin, cackling laugh. "That's the way it is. I got me that mine, and it's done right good by me, if I do say so."

"Ain't you scared somebody'll steal it while you're way down here?"

"Nobody's a-going to find *my* little mine! I got her hid so well nobody could find her. . . . Nobody, that is, except you."

"Me?"

Gabe nodded. "Last couple of years my rheumatiz plumb got the best of me. Couldn't work my mine no more so I went to Denver, changed my dust into money in the bank, and I come out here to live. I been a-wondering what to do with that claim. Last night I got to thinking. Who else'd be better to give it to than my best friend's son?" He handed John an official looking paper and a small map.

"But I can't take it from you for nothing and I ain't got the money to buy it."

"There ain't no problem with you a-taking it for free. I can't work it no more myself. . . . I ain't rich, but I ain't a-worrying about what I'll need for the rest of my life, so I ain't fixing to sell it. I want ya to have it, John!"

They argued about it for awhile, but John finally gave in and accepted it.

"It's plumb easy to find. Go to Red Cedar on the eastern slope of the Rockies and ride up Buffalo Creek till ya come to my cabin. . . . " He pointed to the paper in John's hand. "Here, I drawed ya a map that'll show it, plain as day. Then, when ya find the cabin and have a mind to start a-working the mine, go into the bedroom, take up the loose boards under the bed and go in. That's the opening to my mine. I been a-working that there mine for nigh on to fifteen years and nobody ain't got wise to it yet."

John thanked him. "But I don't know when I'll get that far north," he said.

"You'll get there!" Gabe said confidently. "Leastwise you oughta get there. It'd be worth the trip. Yes, sirree. It'd be worth the trip!"

Breckenridge thanked the old man again, put the papers in his saddlebags after Gabe left, and in a few days forgot all about them.

He had been staying at the hotel almost two months when Josiah Snyder and Bruce Todd came back to town. They got there late in the afternoon, took their horses to the stable, and went to the hotel. John was on his way to the dining room when he saw them at the desk. At first he scarcely recognized Snyder. The rancher's hair seemed more gray than before, his shoulders sagged, and dejection and weariness dulled his eyes.

John hurried over to him. "Josiah!" he exclaimed, thrusting out his hand. "It's good to see you."

His employer's expression did not change. "How are ya, John?"

"Getting along great. My leg's as good as ever." He expected some response, but there was none. Slowly he realized there was no warmth in Snyder; he acted as though he didn't care one way or another that John's hip had mended. "How's things with you?" the trail boss asked.

The older man signed the register and threw a coin across the counter. Sims failed to catch it and it rolled to the floor.

"We'll go over to the saloon for a drink, and I'll tell you all about it."

John's eyes reflected his disapproval.

"I don't care whether ya like it or not!" Snyder exploded. "I'm going for a drink!"

"Let's eat first."

Reluctantly, the rancher allowed himself to

be persuaded to go into the dining room with his two companions and have supper before heading for the saloon.

"How'd you get along with the herd?" John asked eagerly.

Snyder lifted his head to glare at the youthful trail boss. "You wanta know what we got out of them?" he demanded. "Well, I'll tell ya! We didn't get nothing! *Not one red cent!*"

John gasped. "You've got to be joking!"

"That's the truth," Todd broke in. "Snyder was dealing with two or three big buyers when a storm hit. It'd been cold and rainy on us the last couple of weeks of our drive and half of that south-bred herd of ours had the sniffles and was beginning to feel poorly."

John nodded. He had heard other drovers talk about the damage cold weather could do to cattle that weren't used to it.

"Then a two-day blizzard hit—a bad one for that early in the season. The cattle that didn't die was spread all over the territory. We held the drovers for awhile and had them scouring the hills, but we couldn't find nothing but dead ones. . . . " He breathed deeply. "The whole herd was wiped out!"

"That was tough!"

"I finally run outta money and had to sell off the chuck wagon to get enough to get home," Snyder put in.

"I'm right sorry to hear that."

"And that ain't all. I've got a mortgage on the Walking S that's supposed to be paid when we get back." Snyder stared beyond his companions. "Where I missed my bet was in not taking up that oily little dude LeFleur's offer in Abilene. He offered to get me a swear paper so's I could sell my herd in Chicago. I had a chance to come out, but I didn't take it. Now, look what happened!" He gestured helplessly.

"You wouldn't have done that," John told him. "You ain't that kind of a man."

Snyder's mouth quivered. "Just try me," he snarled. "Give me a chance at a shot like that again."

18

Snyder and Todd went from the hotel dining room to the saloon as soon as they finished supper. They asked John to join them but made no effort to persuade him to change his mind when he refused.

"See that you're ready in the morning," the rancher said. "We'll be on our way before daylight."

John's gaze met his. "See that you're *able* to go."

Snyder's ruddy cheeks flushed and for an instant young Breckenridge saw hostility flash in the other man's eyes.

"Don't worry about me. I can take care of myself."

When they were gone, John went to tell the Norvall family good-bye. If Snyder left at the time he said, there would be no opportunity to thank Matt, Rebecca, and the girls for taking care of him.

They knew he would be leaving soon, but Helen was disturbed that he would be going the next day. "Do you have to?"

"I reckon so."

"But we ain't finished our book yet. You won't ever know how it ends."

He smiled. "Guess I'll have to come back so's we can take care of that. OK?"

Her young features brightened. "I'll leave a marker in our place."

He reached over and rumpled her hair.

That last night with Matt and his family reminded him of that evening a few years before when he was ready to leave home—only this was a little easier. He thought highly of them, but he wasn't deceiving anyone as he had Waddy and Miriam. They knew he was going. When it finally came time for him to return to his room, Matt followed him.

"If you ever have need of a job, stop around."

Spending the rest of his life in the hotel business wasn't to his liking, but he couldn't tell his friend that. He appreciated the friendship of the hotel owner and the offer he had made. "Thanks," he said. "I'll keep it in mind."

The eastern sky was still black as ebony and Ogallala was asleep when Snyder hammered on John's door. "Let's get with it! We've got to be riding."

"I'll be right there!"

They left the isolated little town and rode south through Nebraska and Kansas. Snyder was obsessed with the thought that he could have gotten a fake swear paper in Abilene that would have allowed him to sell his herd for shipment to Chicago.

"I'll never make another mistake like that again," he growled. "If I'd only been half smart I could've hired LeFleur and sold those critters for so much I'd have had to buy one of them new wagons they've started building in Montana—the ones with a false floor to make a place to hide the gold so's the thieves couldn't find it. As it is I'm going home flat busted." He thought about Belle's death and began to feel sorry for himself. "I've already lost my wife, and when my mortgage comes due I'll lose the Walking S and what cattle I've got left." He swore bitterly. "All because I was too dumb to take up a good thing while I had the chance."

"You'll make it back, Josiah," John said with confidence he really didn't feel.

"And just how am I supposed to do that?" Snyder demanded, irritated by the quick assurance his trail boss expressed.

"I don't know, but you will."

"That's a sight easier to say than it is to do."

Frost had been in the air when they left Ogallala, but by the time they reached Texas the beauty of fall was upon them. The rays of the sun were smiling pleasantly upon the trio of weary riders. The fall rains had started and the grass that had been brown and lifeless as tinder took on a lush green hue, making the Spanish sword and cacti look pale and ailing. The water holes that had been dry for much of the summer were full again.

They were almost home when another change came over Snyder. A new hope gleamed in his eyes and some of his former optimism and excitement showed through the gloom.

"What's come over you, Josiah?" Todd wanted to know. "You act like you'd found a goldmine!"

"I just figgered how I'm a-going to save the Walking S," he said. "I don't want you two to shuck out and take other jobs till I talk to the banker. If he'll go along with me just once more, I'll be a-needing both of you for next year."

That surprised John. "Are you fixing to take another herd north?"

"Wait till I see what the bank says. Then I'll tell ya."

The week after the weary trio reached the Snyder spread, the rancher rode in to Tucupido to see the banker. Snyder was supposed to return home that night but he didn't show up for three days. And when he came riding in it was obvious that he had been on a drinking binge. His eyes were bloodshot and his face florid and swollen. There was a long, jagged cut along one cheekbone and a purple knot on his jaw. John knew what had happened but said nothing. He held Snyder's horse while the rancher dismounted uncertainly and started for the house. He had staggered almost to the backdoor when Todd came out to meet him.

"Well," the hand exclaimed, "did ya see him?"

Snyder scowled. "None of your business!"

Surprised by the venom in his voice Todd backed off. "I was a-wondering if you seen him and got things worked out."

The rancher pushed past his loyal friend, stormed into the kitchen, and threw his big frame into a chair at the table.

"Turned you down, didn't he?" John asked.

Snyder planted both hands on the table and lifted himself half out of the chair. "No!" he roared. "He didn't turn me down!" He settled back into the chair and stared into space. "To tell you the truth," he said, his voice quivering, "I felt a might shaky a-going into the bank to talk with him about extending that mortgage for another year, so I went into the saloon to get a little shot to quiet my nerves. A couple of my friends was there and we had two or three more. Anyway, I wasn't in no shape to talk to no banker. . . . I reckon I'll have to see him later."

A few days went by before Snyder saw the banker, outlined his plan, and got the mortgage extended for a year. He returned to the Walking S jubilant over his success.

"I got it!" he told John and the skeleton crew. "When I told him my plan he said it'd work. He was sure enough to string along with me for another year."

"That's real good news," John said.

"It is for a fact. Now, we've got work to do. It's a-going to take a little time to get another herd together."

Although April and the day they were to leave for the north were still a few months away, Snyder started hiring men. That, in itself, seemed strange to John, with money as tight as it was around the Walking S. And the caliber of the new men was disturbing. Most of the drovers on previous drives were ordinary cowmen, skilled in handling horses and the unpredictable, ill-tempered longhorns. The new drovers were able to handle themselves in the saddle and soon proved their ability to cut and rope the most stubborn of cattle, but they were a scruffy, hard-bitten lot. Their guns hung low on their hips and their eyes were as cold as the Montana blizzard that had robbed the rancher of his last herd. John didn't say anything about them, however, until the Haynes brothers, Elim and Little Ike, showed up at the Walking S. Snyder had met and hired them in Tucupido. They acted as surprised to see John Breckenridge at the Walking S as he was to see them.

"Corbitt told us how you'd shucked out after the fiasco at the bank in Gladstone," Elim said. "We figgered maybe you'd decided you wasn't dry behind the ears and took off for home."

"We sure enough didn't think you'd be no trail boss," Little Ike cackled.

"And I can't understand why Snyder thinks he needs a couple of fellers like you around the spread," John said.

Elim's lips curled contemptuously, and his voice taunted John. "He can't be too particular. He's got *you* on the payroll!"

John's temper flared, but he resisted the urge to strike back. He remained silent and looked quickly away to keep Elim from seeing his anger. Little Ike saw the tenseness in the moment and moved to get his hot-headed older brother away before trouble erupted.

He touched Elim on the shoulder. "Let's get our gear into the bunkhouse and take care of our horses."

John watched as they slipped their bedrolls and saddlebags from the backs of their mounts and went into the bunkhouse. Moments later they returned, loosed their horses, and went past young Breckenridge on their way to the barn.

"You stay out of my way, kid," Elim warned under his breath.

"I was about to tell you the same thing!"

They glared at each other, but Little Ike called to his brother. Elim turned hesitantly, and the moment of danger passed.

As the sun's rays were bearing down on John, he wiped the sweat from his forehead with the back of his powerful hand and started toward the house. He couldn't imagine Snyder hiring the Haynes brothers without knowing what manner of men they were. Their characters were stamped indelibly on their rough, seamed features. Even though he was sure the rancher knew, he had to warn him.

Snyder was sitting at the kitchen table, poring over a big map when John entered. Snyder was concentrating on it intently and didn't realize anyone was in the room until spurs rattled noisily on the rough floor. Startled, he jerked erect.

"John!" he exploded, fumbling nervously with the map in his haste to get it folded and out of his trail boss's sight. "What're you a-doing here?"

"I come to see you."

The rancher's face purpled. "Don't you know enough to knock?"

"I ain't never knocked before!"

"From now on, knock. Just because you're trail boss don't give you cause to come busting in here any time ya feel like it!"

Angrily, John whirled and started out.

"Where'd you think you're going?" Snyder demanded.

"Back to the bunkhouse."

"You come to see me about something, out with it! What'd you want that was so all-fired important you stormed in here without knocking?"

Reluctantly, Breckenridge turned back. "I just came in to talk to you about them two new men."

Snyder's eyes narrowed. "What about them?"

"You know anything about Little Ike and Elim Haynes?"

"I know they can ride and herd cattle."

John cleared his throat. He didn't like informing on the new men. He had always figured a man's past was his own business, but the way things had been going for the owner of the Walking S he felt that he had to let Snyder know so he could be watching them. "I happen to know they're outlaws. They were in a gang that knocked off a bank in Colorado quite a spell back."

Snyder was breathing heavily and John saw his eyes darken. "What's that to you?"

"Nothing. I just figgered you ought to know so as you could keep your eyes open."

Snyder got to his feet, staring hard across the table at his young trail boss. "Well, now I know!" he retorted irritably. "So if you ain't got nothing else to say, go out and leave me alone."

Breckenridge went back to the bunkhouse and stretched out on his cot. One of these days, he told himself bitterly, Snyder was going to blow up once too often. He didn't have to stay on the Walking S. He could get a job on one of the other spreads in the neighborhood or head for Montana Territory and work the claim old Gabe had given him. Most anything would be better than putting up with the ill-tempered rancher; only he had promised Belle he'd stay with Snyder as long as he wanted him.

The Haynes brothers came in presently and saw John on his bunk, but they ignored him as though he weren't there. And, after a time, Todd entered. He made his way to the rear of the building and sat on a cot next to John's.

"See them two Snyder hired?" he asked softly.

Breckenridge nodded.

"He's a-getting worse-looking drovers every day. I'd hate to go to sleep around here at night if I had something one of them wanted. They look like they could shoot a body, quick as look at him."

John swung his feet over the side of the bunk and sat up. "There's something a-bothering me." He was still talking little above a whisper. "Why's Snyder a-looking at a map of Mexico?"

A strange light flecked Todd's eyes. "I didn't know he was."

John realized his companion was lying, but he didn't want to make an issue of it. "When I went in the house just now he was studying a map of Mexico."

Todd got up abruptly. "I wouldn't worry about it if I was you. It wouldn't concern you none."

"He ain't figgering on raiding Mex cattle like some of the others has done?"

Todd answered him with a question. "You don't think the boss'd do that?"

"I wouldn't have thought so six months ago," John replied. "Now I wouldn't know."

"Just forget it! As far as I know, there ain't nothing going on you wouldn't approve of."

John stared after him. He didn't know why Todd would say what he did if Snyder wasn't planning on raiding a big hacienda south of the border, but he couldn't confront Snyder with it. He would be fired on the spot.

Yet he wasn't riding for an outfit that was rustling, even though most of the Texas ranchers in the area didn't count raids into Mexico as stealing. It was an accepted method of building up one's herd. And it was comparatively safe. Once the cattle were across the border, the Mexicans weren't apt to follow and the authorities in Texas usually looked the other way.

He was still considering the problem when he drifted to sleep that night. He didn't want to quit; he still felt a sense of responsibility to the graying rancher in spite of the change that had come over him and the thinly veiled hostility he sometimes showed towards John. Besides, there was Breckenridge's promise to Belle. He had to do what he could to help, as long as that help didn't take him on the other side of the law.

The following morning Snyder came to the bunkhouse before breakfast and told John he wanted him to check the cattle.

"Wahl just had a hand look them over three or four days ago," Breckenridge answered.

"I know!" he retorted irritably. "But I want them checked again! And if you work for me ya do what I tell you to. Understand?"

John nodded.

"I bought some longhorns down in Mexico last week. I'm a-going to take Wahl and some of the boys down to get them."

"You *bought* them?" John asked. He hadn't intended to say that. The words just popped out.

"I *bought* them!" Snyder's temper flared. "You calling me a liar?"

"I ain't calling you nothing. But that ain't the way most of the cattle get here from Mexico."

"Well, that's the way these're a-coming. But if you don't believe me, you can hit the road."

John pushed his hat lower over his eyes and started for the door.

"I'll begin checking the herd this morning," he said.

"That's better. And see that ya watch your tongue! You keep a-talking like you did just now and you'll get yourself in big trouble."

Snyder and the Walking S hands he took with him were gone a week. When they returned, they were driving three-hundred-fifty head of the scrawniest longhorns John had ever seen.

"It's going to take some time and mighty good grass to get them cattle in shape to start north," he told the rancher.

"That's why we got them now." He was jubilant. "They'll be in shape come April."

"Them cattle's wearing a Mexican brand," John said.

"You accusing me of rustling?"

Breckenridge had gone this far; he had to continue. "It looks strange, Josiah. You being outta money and all. Then ya leave for a week and come back with a herd of longhorns. A man can't help wondering."

The muscles in Snyder's face tightened as he fought for self-control. "If Belle hadn't taken such a shine to you, so help me, I'd blow you away!"

"Don't let that stop you!"

Snyder swore and turned on his heel. "Come to the house. You ain't a-going to be satisfied till you see the bill of sale."

John followed him, hoping that Snyder actually had the paper he said he did. They went through the kitchen to the bedroom that also served as an office.

"Here it is!" he growled, shoving a piece of paper in John's hands. "Course it's written in Spanish, so ya don't really know if it's what I say it is. . . . Take it to Tucupido and get one of them Mexicans to read it to you—iffen you can find one who can read."

"I'll take your word for it."

Later, when John was riding herd on the new cattle he began to wonder. He had no doubt that the paper said what Snyder claimed it did, but he could've gotten one of those same Mexicans he was talking about to write out the paper for a bottle of tequila or a couple of dollars. Yet John had to trust him until he found out differently.

During the next few months the owner of the Walking S visited every rancher in the area, offering to take their saleable stock to market in the north for half of the amount they would get for them. It made a better deal than selling in Texas where there seemed to be more cattle than people, or taking the time to take a herd north themselves. Before he finished he had a herd as big as the last one. It began to look as though John had been right in saying Snyder would soon be on top again.

Late in February the rancher went to Tucupido and had a government wagon worked over for a chuck wagon. It had axles of iron and a can of tallow in the place where a tar bucket was usually carried. On the other side there was a water barrel for cooking and drinking. There was a hinged lid at the back of the wagon, supported by a swinging leg that could be put down to allow Cookie to have a worktable. There were shelves and drawers for the staples and a box for the tin tableware, cups, and plates, as well as the smaller cast-iron utensils carried on the drive. The drovers' bedrolls were carried up front, along with a bag or two of oats for the horses pulling the chuck wagon.

When they were getting ready to leave with the herd, John figured the time had come for him to use his pa's Colt. He had grown five inches and gained twenty-five pounds since he had bought the Smith and Wesson a few years back. He unstrapped the .32 and put on the Colt Peacemaker.

"That's a real gun," Little Ike Haynes sneered. "Think you can handle it?"

"Any time you want to find out, just say the word."

Early in April, a cold, wet wind brought out the long, yellow slickers, as Snyder and the drovers moved the herd out of the Walking S pasture where they were being held. This time the rancher told John he wasn't going to waste any time and run the risk of getting caught in another Montana blizzard. "If we have to go that way," he added.

"What do you mean by that?"

"You are the suspicious one, ain't you? If ya have to know, I've been a-thinking we might be able to sell our herd to the army or some rancher in Colorado or Wyoming . . . if that's all right with you." Sarcasm was heavy in his voice.

John turned Rusty and rode away, his back hunched miserably against the rain and battering wind.

The going was slow and cheerless as the rain continued for two weeks. The cattle were stubborn and determined to lag behind or dart off for some nearby clump of brush they could use for shelter. The drovers spent long hours in the saddle, forgetting what it was to be dry and warm, till they stopped for the dark hours to have their second meal of the day before tumbling into their tarp-protected bedrolls. They had to take turns riding herd at night, of course, but they didn't complain. They knew when they signed on that the hours would be long and tortuous.

Reaching the Red River, they were faced with taking the herd across the rain-swollen stream. John Breckenridge and Bruce Todd wanted to wait until the river crested and started down, but Snyder wouldn't hear of it. He was driving both men and cattle as one possessed, making sure they reached the stopping point he had chosen for each night before they made camp.

"It's a-going to be dangerous for the cattle and drovers and their horses," John protested.

"If anybody's scared, they can get their pay," the rancher flared. "And that includes you!"

The crossing was even worse than John had anticipated. It was difficult to force the wily longhorns into the water and equally hard to keep them from drifting down stream with the powerful current. The flood water was deeper than an animal could wade and they had to swim, another factor that increased the problems.

Midway in the crossing, one of the hands who had dismounted and was hanging to the tail of his swimming horse, was bumped by a panicked longhorn. He lost his grip and went down. Helplessly, John and Snyder watched from the bank as the drover's head and arms came up momentarily. He flailed about in the water, but without success. He went down again and that was the last they saw of him.

As soon as the herd was across the river, Breckenridge left Todd in charge and rode down stream for several miles, looking for the drover's body. He came back hours later, deeply disturbed by the accident and the loss of one of his men.

"We're a-going to be short-handed," he told Snyder. "We'll have to pick up another drover or two as soon as we can."

The rancher smiled bleakly. "We don't have nothing to worry about on that score. I'll ride ahead to Abilene and see what I can find."

"Abilene?" John exclaimed. "I thought we was a-going to Dodge."

"I changed my mind."

"You're figgering on dealing with LeFleur, ain't you?"

Snyder's eyes blazed. "You're being paid to drive cattle. *I'll* do the thinking!"

"If ya do, you'd better find another man to take my place."

"I already got one," the rancher snarled. He rode off, abruptly cutting off the conversation. He stayed away from John till they neared the Kansas border. Then he approached the trail boss and told him he was going to Abilene.

"How long till you get back?" he asked.

"I'll be gone as long as it takes."

John knew what that meant. He might be gone an extra week or two weeks. It all depended on how thirsty he happened to be.

That evening, however, Snyder and two new drovers approached from the north. There was no mistaking the rancher or the blue-roan he rode. Bruce Todd was the first to notice them.

"Ain't that Snyder a-coming?" he asked, pointing at the riders in the distance.

"Sure enough," John said. "He didn't go all the way to Abilene."

"He must've got some new men in Caldwell."

John stared at the trio. There was something familiar about them, particularly the man next to Snyder. He sat his horse ramrod straight, like a professional soldier. There was only one rider the young trail boss knew who looked like that in the saddle; but it couldn't be him!

Curiously John touched Rusty with the spurs and rode forward. His eyes rounded and he breathed rapidly. It couldn't be Lee Corbitt; but it was! And he looked no different than the last time John had seen him. Even more surprising, Obed Metzner was along.

John's first impulse was to ride forward and greet them. Then he remembered that Elim and

Little Ike were already riding with the herd. Now Lee's old gang was complete, or what was left of it! And they were with the trail herd. Why . . . *Why?*

19

John waited for the trio to ride up. Corbitt reined in as soon as he recognized the young trail boss. His features went taut and John thought he saw an almost imperceptible move toward his gun.

"Hello, John. It's been a long time."

"That it has."

"It's good to see you, kid," Obed said.

John nodded. An icy weakness gripped his stomach until he thought he would be sick.

"I see you know each other," Snyder broke in curiously.

"We rode together some years back," Corbitt told him.

"Now you're riding together again. John's my trail boss."

The silence that followed was taut with emotion. Snyder realized something was wrong and wanted to get the new drovers away from John.

"Todd," he ordered, "take these men to the remuda and have them pick out some hosses that ain't been rode."

"Ain't no hurry about that, Mr. Snyder," Corbitt said.

"Todd'll be riding flank tomorrow. Better get them hosses picked out today."

When they were gone the rancher turned to John.

"What was that all about?" he asked.

"Something personal."

"It ain't personal iffen it affects my moving this herd. . . . There's bad blood between you and them two. I want to know what it's about."

John hesitated. "I run out on him," he said, "after he warned me not to."

"That's all you're a-going to tell me?"

"That's all I'm a-going to tell you."

"I hired them in a saloon in Caldwell," Snyder continued. "I don't figger on letting them go just because you don't happen to like them."

"I never said I wanted them fired. All I can say is watch them. Watch them real close."

The rancher's eyes flashed. "I don't want to hear no more of that!"

He rode off to return his mount to the remuda. For a time John stared motionless after his boss. Why had they signed on with the trail herd? They weren't the kind to be drovers; Corbitt especially. He was used to a softer life than that. And Elim and Little Ike were around. With them on the drive, too, they had to have something planned. Something like stealing the herd or beating the rancher out of the little money he had left. He was still watching Snyder when Todd came up.

"So you know them characters."

"I know them."

"Sounds as if you don't think much of them."

"I don't trust them. They're sidekicks of the Haynes boys."

Todd whistled his amazement. "You sure of that?"

"I ought to be. I was with them for awhile."

"Snyder know about this?"

John frowned. "You know how he is these days. You can't tell him nothing."

Todd dismounted and led his horse to the shade of a gnarled cottonwood. "If something happens, it'll be his own fault," he said.

"I just don't want nothing to happen."

Todd kicked a cow chip carelessly. "I thought maybe Snyder'd get one of them swear papers from LeFleur and we'd be done with this drive, but no such luck. Guess we're going to have to take the herd all the way to Wyoming or Montana."

John had been wondering about LeFleur and if there would have to be a showdown between himself and Snyder on account of the Frenchman.

"What about LeFleur?"

"Didn't Snyder tell ya?" Todd said. "The vigilantes caught him slipping out of Abilene about a month ago and hanged him. He won't be getting swear papers for nobody any more."

John didn't know whether they were acting or not, but the Haynes brothers seemed as surprised as he was to see Corbitt and Obed. They talked some in general terms, but there was a coolness between them.

The following morning shortly after daylight, they started to move the herd again, this time in a different direction. They went west toward Dodge City and beyond, to the trail that led up to Montana. The sun had broken through the lowering, moisture-laden clouds, and, with the help of a gentle breeze, drove the clouds away. With the warmth of spring upon them everyone felt better. Even the ugly tempered longhorns, who seemed to carry a grudge against every other living creature and especially the drovers, stepped out briskly, causing minimal trouble.

They made their way over grass that had suddenly drawn new life from the rains and was lush and green. In the days that followed it seemed that the rib-showing cattle from Mexico were putting on flesh in spite of the rigors of the drive. And Snyder, who had been morose and silent for most of the trip, was cheered by the progress they were making. He took to sitting with the drovers around the fire at night, swapping stories and laughing expansively.

John kept to himself, avoiding Corbitt and Obed as much as possible. They were not anxious to be around him, either. The herd was driven west across an Indian reserve where they lost a dozen critters to the arrows of braves who were trying to exact a fee from Snyder for the grass his cattle ate. From there they angled northwest into Colorado.

There were several days of rain again and another swollen stream to cross, but that time all went well. John was pleased with the progress they were making and thought Snyder would be pleased, as well. But a change had come over him. He was in one of those dark moods that had become so common through the winter months. He withdrew from the men and ate and rode alone. He was restless and irritable; the way he usually got before going on a drinking binge. John recognized the symptoms and was disturbed. Fortunately, the whiskey Snyder had brought back from Caldwell was already gone, but there was yet another threat. They were nearing the town of Box Butte in Colorado, and somebody would have to go in to replenish their supplies. John had to keep the rancher away from town if he could.

When they reached the point closest to Box

Butte and the town by the same name at its base, Breckenridge sought out Snyder and told him he was going to take Cookie and the chuck wagon to town the next morning for supplies.

The rancher frowned. "I was figgering on making that trip myself," he blurted defensively.

"I can do it for you," the trail boss answered.

Snyder glared at him, reading the disapproval in the young man's eyes and resenting it. "What is this, kid?" he demanded contemptuously, a sneer marring his voice. "You telling me you're taking over?"

"I figgered I'd save you the trip."

"Let me do the figgering around here! That's my job. And when I say I'm a-going to town I don't want no back talk outta you!"

John knew the reason for Snyder's anger and realized it was useless to talk with him. The rancher had made up his mind to go to town, and the first place he stopped would be the saloon. John started to turn away, but Snyder stopped him.

"I ain't done with you yet," he snarled belligerently. "You're a-getting too big for your britches, and I ain't taking no back talk. I'm plumb tired of having you think you can boss me around the way Belle used to."

"I wasn't bossing you," John protested. He tried to sound calm and conciliatory, but he was so exasperated that his own frustration and anger showed through. The rancher saw this, and his temper flared and exploded bitterly.

"Are ya calling me a liar?" he cried, quivering with rage. "Nobody calls me a liar! Get your gear and move out. You're fired!"

"If that's the way you want it, fine. Give me my time and I'll be outta here in an hour!"

225

Snyder ripped the wallet from his pocket and counted out the money he owed his trail boss. "An hour's twice too long to suit me!"

John jammed the bills into his pocket, stormed over to the chuck wagon, and ordered Cookie to get his bedroll for him.

"What's going on?" the cook asked, grinning.

"None of your business!"

Cookie's cheeks flushed. "You don't need to get so uppity! I was just wondering."

"Keep your wondering to yourself!"

John had tied his bedroll to the back of his saddle and was mounting Rusty when Corbitt and Obed rode up. "Just talked to the boss," Corbitt said. "He tells me you ain't a-working for him no more."

"I was a-getting tired of taking his guff anyway."

There was a short, taut silence. "We'll be up to Montana to see you and that claim of yours," Corbitt said.

John's gaze hardened. "What're you talking about?"

"We figgered we'd stop by after we get paid off and talk over old times. Didn't we, Obed?"

"For a fact!"

"You don't need to tell us how to get there," Corbitt continued. "We've got a map!"

John's temper flared. He would have pushed the matter further, but Snyder was glaring at him, and he knew that time had run out. He had to leave or have a confrontation with his former boss that he might be sorry about later.

Without saying more he mounted Rusty and rode off in the direction of Red Cedar, Montana Territory, and Buffalo Creek. He was still smarting under the arrogant words of Lee Corbitt. That had been no careless slip of the tongue; it had been deliberate. They were letting him know they had searched his saddlebags and had taken the map—telling him they would be after him to square accounts and try to get to Gabe's claim at the same time. Fortunately, he remembered the crude drawing and would have no difficulty finding the claim. The run-in with Corbitt added to the bitter anger of Snyder's assault and for several miles he rode Rusty hard. He splashed across a narrow creek without slowing, galloped up a steep sage-covered hill, and rode along the crest a quarter of a mile. The big sorrel's withers were lathered a dirty white, and his chest was heaving as he fought to do his master's will. Only then did the rider seem to come to his senses: He reined in and dismounted.

"That's all right, boy," he said, patting his horse on the neck. "Catch your breath and cool down a little. We ain't in that big a hurry. We'll take it easy from now on."

He sat on the ground near his horse, arms wrapped about his knees, looking off into the distance at the luxuriant green prairie stretching to the horizon; yet he scarcely noted its beauty. He was breathing almost as heavily as the big sorrel, but for a different reason. Anger at Snyder had quickened his pulse and caused his lungs to labor; like Rusty he had to cool down.

After a time the sweat dried on his mount and Rusty was breathing normally. He began to graze on the buffalo grass that carpeted the hill between the sage and yucca.

"Time to go," John said, gathering the reins and stepping into the saddle to ride off at a brisk walk. "We've got us a long trip before we reach Montana Territory."

At the next stream he stopped, watered Rusty, and let him graze for an hour. He was in no hurry. Box Butte was his destination and that was only a few miles away. He would get a haircut, a bath, and a good bed before buying the grub he needed for the trip north.

Snyder would also be on his way to town. If he had taken the shortcut the scout had explained to John, it was likely he would already be there. Breckenridge wondered if he would see the rancher in Box Butte; maybe they would run into each other. If they did, he wondered what the burly rancher would say, now that he had had time to cool down. He might apologize and ask John to come back. He had been known to do that when he was drunk. Should that happen John wondered what his own response would be. There was no denying it; he enjoyed many things about being trail boss, sizing up the challenge before him and devising ways of meeting it. There was excitement in guiding the herd and drovers on their way north—an excitement he would miss.

Yet, working for Snyder had not been easy. It had been different before Belle died; she was a leveling influence on the big, impetuous, unstable rancher. She was the one who had kept him straight and moving toward his goals. She had handled him so deftly he hadn't even been aware of it most of the time.

Being fired irked John, but in some ways he was glad to be rid of his responsibilities. Now he didn't have to concern himself with whether the Mexican cattle had been stolen or legally bought and paid for, or if Snyder would try something else—like his plan to buy a phony swear paper so he could get the herd to the Chicago market. With a man like Snyder there was no telling what to expect. John wasn't positive, but he didn't think he would go back to the herd, even if he had the opportunity.

Josiah Snyder was already in town when John rode in and stabled Rusty at the livery barn. Snyder's horse was there and so was Todd's. John supposed they were at the saloon; that was the first place they usually headed. Well, let them stay there! He sure wasn't going to hunt them up and try to get Snyder sober. He had had enough of that when he was on the payroll.

He walked over to the barbershop beside Box Butte's only hotel, got cleaned up, and had a haircut. Then he went next door, rented a room, and made his way to the café for the first decent meal he had had since they hit the trail. The next morning when he went back to get his horse the Walking S horses were still there. That meant Snyder and Todd were also still in town.

"They can stay for a week, for all I care," he muttered to himself as he mounted the big sorrel and cantered up the wide street, turning north at the edge of town.

Traveling on horseback alone was faster by far than being with the herd. Every day he covered as much ground as the longhorns could manage in four or five or even a week, if the herd was cantankerous. He left Colorado and rode into Wyoming Territory toward the end of the second day. He would not be far from Weaverville and home, he realized, and at first was almost overwhelmed by the desire to stop and see Waddy Ross and Miriam. It had been four years since he had left the Rocking Seven. But he could not do that. Fletch would be sure to ask what he had been doing, and when he learned that he had left the Snyder herd halfway to Montana he would pry him with questions until he learned about the firing.

No, John decided, he would go on to Montana and work the claim for awhile. Then, if he still wanted to, he would come back to the ranch.

After ten days on the trail John reached Red Cedar, bought some tools, a box of dynamite, and laid in a supply of grub. The clerk in the general store eyed him curiously but asked no questions. It was not the way of the west to pry. A man was accepted for what he was. The clerk would know from his purchases that he was prospecting, but unless the area was different than any other in the hills he knew about, there were always those who were looking for the show of color that would make them rich.

John did not remain in town for the night but rode west and north along the trail that led to the mountains and Buffalo Creek. He asked no questions that would give an indication of where he was going, nor did he volunteer any information.

Several miles out of town he unsaddled Rusty and made camp for the night, building a small, smokeless fire that would not give his presence away. But it was a desolate stretch of country and no one came by. At dawn he saddled his mount and rode on. Shortly after noon he reached Buffalo Creek.

Here he was careful to hide the horse's tracks. He didn't want anyone to see them and get to wondering why a shod animal would have been going that direction. It would be a way of getting unexpected and unwanted company. Of course nothing he could do would keep Corbitt and Obed from coming; they had the map Gabe had made for him. They would be along, sooner or later, and when that happened, he would have to be ready for them.

John cut a few branches from the willows along the stream and brushed out the horse's hoofprints. A few hours of wind teasing the sand or a sprinkling of rain and the brush marks would disappear, effectively hiding his presence in the area.

Before the sun was behind the peaks to the west, John had reached the neat little cabin along the rushing waters of the creek. He remained astride his horse momentarily, taking in the scene. Old Gabe had been right: It was breath-takingly beautiful. Even if there were no gold it would be a great place to stay.

20

John unsaddled his sorrel, curried him, and rubbed
him down. Rusty reveled in the feel of the steel
teeth of the curry comb and the brisk massage of
the brush on his sweating back. By the time John
finished, the big horse had cooled down so it was
safe for him to drink the icy water. When he had
his fill John led him to a small pasturelike piece
of ground containing an acre or so of good grass.
It lay hard against a rocky spire that thrust a
hundred feet toward the sky and the sheer granite face of a cliff that towered several hundred
feet over the floor of the narrow gorge.

Far above, an eagle wheeled, wings motionless against the azure sky. His sharp eyes were
sweeping the canyon floor for the telltale signs of
a rabbit or gopher that would help fill the gullets
of the pair of eaglets in some high, well-protected
nest. There were trout in the stream at John's
feet, and on the opposite cliff face, halfway to the
ledge, he could make out the forbidding blackness
of a cave. It had a jagged, egg-shaped hole that
looked small from such a distance, but was probably large enough for a man to stand in without
taking off his hat.

Much of the area was well forested with
straight, slim pine, spruce, and the ever-present
aspen that were too soft to be used for anything.

John turned his attention to the cabin the old man had given him. The logs used in its construction had been painstakingly selected and maneuvered to the claim with infinite patience and care. The sides of each pine stick had been shaved with meticulous precision to fit snugly against the other, and notched at the corners to form a sturdy structure.

The floor, roof, and doors were made of handsawed lumber a full inch thick and planed smooth, save for a few teeth marks from the Swede saw that had been used to cut them. These, too, were closely fitted and held in place by hardwood pegs. There may have been nails in the building, but if there were, John didn't see them.

He marveled at the tremendous amount of labor that had gone into the cabin. He didn't know how Gabe could have accomplished so much without outside help. Yet, knowing him the little he did, he was confident the old man had worked alone. He was far too cautious to have brought anyone else to the claim and risked the secret it held.

John went outside and looked around. There were signs of Gabe's trapline everywhere. At least two dozen traps hung on pegs along one wall. A pair of snowshoes was suspended beside them, and stretching boards for furs in a variety of sizes lay on the half ceiling that had obviously been put up for extra storage. Everywhere he looked there was evidence that the cabin was occupied by a trapper, but there was nothing to indicate that he was working a claim.

John was curious about the mine and its opening that was hidden by the log structure, but he resisted the temptation to move the boards in the bedroom floor and start exploring. It was almost dark and he was tired from the long trip. There would be plenty of time to spend in the mine later, when he was fully rested. He fried a generous slab of ham, cooked some beans, and ate by the light of one of Gillette's tallow candles. Once the dishes were done he looked out on Rusty to make sure he was all right, spread the bedroll on the bed, and collapsed. The next thing he knew it was morning.

After checking his horse once more and having breakfast, he looked for the loose boards that Gabe had told him were in the bedroom under the bed. They were not as loose as he had thought they would be, and he went over the floor once and started a second time before he found them.

The hole was twelve or fifteen feet deep, laboriously dug a bucket of sand, clay, and rock at a time, by the same man who had built the cabin. John took a match from the box he carried and lighted the candle. He was about to start down the old ladder when he remembered that it had been in place for many years. He tried to pull it up to look it over carefully but it was so heavy he couldn't manage it. Turning and starting down, he tested each rung before resting his weight on it, but he need not have been concerned. The same care Gabe had used in everything else had been used in the ladder. It was as sturdy and firm as it had been the day it was constructed.

The candle flickered dimly, revealing the rocky sides of the excavation. It was obvious that Gabe had dug it out with his pick and shovel. The marks of his tools were still evident, though the grime of years had dulled them until they were scarcely visible. The floor of the mine had also been formed roughly by the same tools.

There was a tunnel leading off the entrance. While Gabe could have stood erect in it, John was so tall he had to stoop. A few feet into the tunnel he came across the old man's tools. There were several picks and shovels, marked by various stages of use, mute evidence that he had worked the diggings over a long period of time. There were two or three large sheet-steel basins that once had been shiny and new, but now showed the rust of neglect. The basins, made especially for panning gold, were about eighteen inches across the top, with slanting sides about two inches high. The bottom of each was flat and approximately fifteen inches in diameter.

John picked one up with his free hand and stared at it. He wondered how long it had been since Gabe used it to sort the gold from the gravel and rock. On the other side of the pans was a wooden box a quarter filled with dynamite, a box of caps, and a coil of fuse. There was a bottle of quicksilver, marked by the familiar skull and cross bones, a wooden sluice box that was used to make the primary separation of materials before the panning process, and a ball of rusted wire. A box nearby was filled with an assortment of hammers, chisels, and tweezers. Along the opposite wall there were two heavy metal buckets and a wheelbarrow. On the ledge above stood a row of candles.

John wasn't sure he knew what all of those items were for, but he had the tattered book Gabe had given him. He decided to do some reading on mining gold and separating it from the rock and gravel before starting to work. But his curiosity got the best of him, and he took up the newest and sharpest pickax and made his way to the end of the tunnel where he began to loosen pieces of mica and garnet and pyrite, along with ordinary stone.

His body was rock hard from long weeks and months in the saddle, but he soon discovered that swinging a pick worked muscles he didn't know he had. That, and the necessity of working in a stooped position because of the low tunnel roof, made him stop frequently for breath. After a couple of hours of pecking at the rough rock wall at the end of the tunnel, he had a small pile of aggregate, which he took to the entrance in the wheelbarrow. Once he got the ore, the sluice box, and the steel pan outside he sat down with the book on gold mining and began to read.

There was more to the process than he had supposed, and many of the details were difficult to understand. But after he had gone over most of the book twice and some portions three times, he thought he was ready to go to work.

Actually, the process was simple in its purpose. Gold was seldom found in its free state. The problem was to separate it from everything else; the ore had to be pounded or crushed into small pieces, the smaller the better, and run through a sluice box to wash the color and smaller particles through the sieve. The floor of the trough that carried the small particles away was covered with heavy canvas to help catch the color. And at intervals, one-inch boards or 'riffles' slowed the flow of water and mud and prevented the gold from being washed out of the box with the waste.

But that was only the beginning. When the riffles were filled with sand and garnets and other materials, it was taken out and panned by hand to remove more of the worthless minerals. Large grains and nuggets of gold could be picked up with a good pair of tweezers—or, if they were large enough, with the fingers.

What was left, however, required the presence of quicksilver to pick up the dust and fine particles of color. Half a teaspoonful of mercury was put into the concentrate, the pan was submerged in water and rotated gently to give the quicksilver opportunity to come in contact with the gold and trap it. If the pan was agitated carefully, the quicksilver would slowly come together, forming one lump. Then it could be scraped up with a knife or putty knife and dropped onto a large piece of chamois skin. Twisting the chamois tightly would squeeze out most of the mercury. The rest of the mercury could be removed from the gold by heating the mixture over a very hot fire. There was a warning to heat the mixture outside because the fumes were poisonous.

Early the next morning John carried the sluice box and the ore down by the mountain stream and set to work, placing a small quantity of the ore and water in the box to wash the material through the sieve. He worked carefully, pausing every few moments to examine the substance caught by the riffles.

There were no large pieces of color, but the quicksilver picked up the gold dust, and he processed it. By the end of the morning he had a teaspoon full of gold, which he stored in a small leather pouch with a draw string at the top. He had no idea how much he had earned for the morning's work, but it was exciting to know the trip to Gabe Gillette's mine had not been fruitless.

For several days John labored frantically every

working hour, as though he feared someone might swoop down and take the mine away before he could work it any more. He would dig out a wheelbarrow-load of ore, haul it up to the sluice box, and process it before getting more.

After a week, however, his excitement began to abate. He realized he was wasting a great deal of time with his current work habits and set up a schedule. For a couple of days he grubbed out ore and hauled it to the entrance. Then he used the sluice box, the pan, and quicksilver, finally burning off the last of the mercury to leave the gold.

The days became weeks and the weeks a month while he worked. The little sacks of dust increased in number. Summer began to fade and fall was in the air. The hours of daylight shortened and the wind was harsh, carrying the hint of snow in its teeth. It wouldn't be long until the cold would be upon the hills and working the mine would be impossible.

Snyder should have reached Montana with his herd by this time. That meant Corbitt and Obed would be showing up at the mine. John took to wearing his six-gun while he worked and keeping his rifle close at hand; he had to be ready when they came. He wouldn't get a second chance with the likes of Lee Corbitt—of that he was certain. And he wasn't leaving for the winter until they had their confrontation. Corbitt wanted it; he was going to get it.

He began to think about returning the sluice box and the other tools to the mine, carrying off the last of the rubble from the ore and spreading it to maintain Gabe's carefully guarded secret. He stopped mining, put the equipment back in the mine entrance where he had found it, and was in the final stages of cleaning up around the cabin, when he heard someone approaching.

He heard the frantic pounding of hooves against the hard gravel just beyond his line of vision. Corbitt! It had to be him or Obed. They were the only ones John knew who were aware of the location of the claim. He dropped the shovel, dashed to the cabin where his rifle leaned near the door, and snatched it up. Then he realized Corbitt wouldn't come charging in so noisily. He would approach on cat's feet, hoping to catch his adversary unawares.

Cradling the weapon in his arm, John waited. A moment later a rider on a heavily lathered horse came into view. Instinctively John raised the rifle as the hard-running animal came into view and jerked to a stop.

"Obed!" he cried.

There was no need to ask why the old man had come. He was hunched over the saddle horn and a huge brownish red stain had spread across the back of his shirt around an ugly black hole just below his collar bone. Clotted blood had gathered around the hole and as John stared, a faint scarlet stream oozed out again.

"John!" Obed gasped. "I . . . I. . . . " He swayed in the saddle and Breckenridge sprang forward— but not in time to keep him from falling. The older man slumped to the ground. John cradled him in his arms. For an instant he thought Obed had died, but the gray-haired outlaw stirred and opened his eyes.

"I shouldn't have come here, John, but you and me got on together and I didn't have no place else to go," he mumbled. "I . . . I didn't want to die alone."

"What happened?"

With effort Obed forced himself to speak again. "Corbitt's dead. Little Ike's dead. Elim may be gone, too, for all I know."

"What happened?" John repeated numbly.

"We hit Snyder after he got paid for his cattle, but everything went wrong. Worse than that bank job in Colorado Territory."

"You what?" Breckenridge cried.

"Elim set it up. I didn't like that. I wanted Corbitt to take charge but Elim claimed he knew right where the money'd be and Corbitt went over his plans and helped him some." Obed stopped and coughed weakly.

"Let me get your shirt off and see if I can get the bleeding stopped."

The old man shook his head. "Ain't no use, John. I've bought it! I . . . I just want to talk. . . . I'm real sorry about the posse that's a-follering me."

"You know they'll think I'm in on it, Obed," John reminded him. "Especially Snyder!"

The old man clutched his arm. "I couldn't help it, John! Like I said, I didn't have nowheres else to go and a body don't want to die alone! I . . . I. . . . " He closed his eyes and his breath came in thin, shallow gasps.

John cut away the old man's shirt and underwear, exposing the bullet hole in the back. He had never removed a lead slug before, but he had to try. Fortunately Gabe had some medicine in the cabin.

"I'll get something to clean up this wound," he said. "Won't be gone more than a minute!"

Obed's lips parted, as though to speak, but the words would not come out. His head fell back and he was dead.

John stared at him incredulously. In that moment he realized he had cared a lot for the old man in spite of the sort of life he had lived.

He knew, as well, that Obed's warning about the posse was true. Snyder would be a wild man, and it would be like him to blame his former trail boss. Lately he had to have someone to accuse for causing every problem and trouble that came his way.

John went down in the mine, got the shovel, and started to dig a shallow grave some distance from the creek. He would have to leave as quickly as he could to avoid the posse, but he was going to bury Obed first. He couldn't leave his body to be torn apart by the wolves.

His heart was aching as he carried Obed to the grave and filled it in. Then he took off his hat and prayed over the grave. He had never prayed before, that he could remember, but he couldn't bury the old man without *some* kind of a service, however brief and casual.

Hurriedly he loaded his gear on Rusty, took a quick trip about the place to be sure he had left nothing, locked the cabin, and rode off, trailing Obed's horse behind him. There was only one way out of the narrow canyon. If the posse was close behind Obed, he might run into them before he reached the main trail. But he didn't worry about that. He would solve the problem if he came to it.

Rusty hadn't been ridden hard for several weeks and was eager to run, but John held him to a brisk canter. The time might come, and soon, when he would need all the speed and stamina the big horse could give.

John knew he should not be running from the posse. The best thing was to wait for them, showing by his presence that he had nothing to hide. When they came he could explain that he had nothing to do with the attempted robbery, that he had been at the cabin all the time. With anyone other than Snyder, that is what he would have done, but it would be his word against Snyder's, and he knew how vindictive and convincing the rancher could be. Breckenridge wouldn't have a chance of proving his innocence. Snyder would be all for stringing him up to the nearest tree. So he had to ride, to get away from there as quickly as possible.

Going back down the creek was faster than going up had been. At the main trail he paused briefly. Corbitt had taught him something when they had been running from the posse after the bank robbery in Gladstone. If they were actually looking for him, doubling back might throw them off. With that as his purpose he turned Rusty in the direction of Red Cedar and rode several miles along the trail before making his way into the hills.

Again he stopped long enough to brush out the big sorrel's tracks for a hundred yards or so. A skilled tracker might not be deceived, but the posse might not be watching closely for hoofprints coming out of the hills, or he might get a little help from the weather. It was worth the time it took to try to hide the direction he had gone.

John found a secluded spot beyond the first ridge where he made camp. There was plenty of water, and he was far enough from the trail so the smoke from his fire would not give him away. He stayed there a week, waiting for the hunt to cool. He had already made up his mind what to do: He was going back to Weaverville—back to the Rocking Seven.

21

John made his way slowly into Weaverville, past the bank and barbershop. It had been several days' ride from Montana Territory to the little town near the Rocking Seven, and both he and the big sorrel needed a rest. It was late in the afternoon, and the crowd at the saloon was growing. The hitching rail in front was lined with horses and several were tied at the rail along the side. He could hear the expressionless patter of the player piano as he rode by.

He half expected to see Waddy's rig in front of Roy Ingerton's General Store, but if it was there he didn't recognize it. There was a buckboard and a spring wagon in front, and Roy and his clerk were hauling supplies out to them. John was about to call out to Ingerton and wave when the storekeeper turned and waddled back inside. The opportunity was gone.

John was on the outskirts of the dusty little town when he decided to go back to the barbershop for a bath, a haircut, and a shave. He wheeled Rusty around abruptly and retraced his steps, half expecting someone to recognize either him or his horse. But that didn't happen. Even as he entered the barbershop a customer on the way out shouldered past without any indication of recognition.

"Stranger in town?" the barber asked as John crawled into the chair after having a bath and getting into clean clothes.

"Not exactly."

"Ain't seen you around." He lathered John's face and stropped the razor. "Course I ain't been here all that long, myself. Moved here a couple a years ago after Enos Martin cashed in." He began to draw the blade over Breckenridge's cheek, chuckling to himself. "Guess I could have married his widow and got the place for nothing, but I figgered that was too high a price." He laughed again.

John didn't feel like talking. All he wanted was to have the barber finish and let him out of the chair. Now that he was so close to Waddy's ranch he could hardly wait. As soon as his hair was cut and the cloth taken from his neck, he pulled a couple of coins from his pocket, got his change, and strode out.

For some reason he hadn't been able to picture the trail from Weaverville to the Rocking Seven, no matter how hard he tried. Now that he was on it again it came rushing back. Every hill, every gully, and every turn was stamped indelibly on his mind. It was almost as though someone had taken a series of tin types and was showing them to him in sequence, one after another.

Despite the fact that he had been in the saddle since dawn, he raked Rusty lightly with the spurs, urging him into a lively canter. Almost before he realized it, he was so close he saw the shadowy outline of the ranch house with smoke spiraling from the chimney.

"There it is!" he said aloud, and it seemed as though he had never been away. He spoke sharply to his mount and leaned forward. The tired horse broke into a gallop.

Miriam heard him ride into the yard and opened the door, letting a narrow, yellow wedge of lamplight fall on the ground in front of the house. Briefly she stared at the horse and rider in the semidarkness, as though she could not quite believe what she was seeing. Then she squealed in delight. "John!" she cried. *"It's John!"* She dashed forward as he climbed off his horse.

"It's good to see you, Miriam," he said. He swept her into his arms and swung her around.

Waddy Ross and Fletcher were two steps behind her. Waddy hurried as fast as his arthritic legs and his cane would allow him to move. Fletch came reluctantly, hanging back, a scowl deepening the lines on his face.

"John!" Waddy took the young man's hand in his own powerful fist and squeezed it savagely. "It's right good to see ya, boy!"

"It's good to see you, too, Pa!"

Waddy released John's hand and turned to his son. "Fletch!" he said, sternly. "Ain't ya going to speak to your brother?"

"Soon as you and Miriam get through."

John held out his hand and Fletch took it reluctantly. Breckenridge couldn't help noting that he towered above his older stepbrother by a head and must have outweighed him by twenty pounds. He wouldn't have to worry about Fletch picking on him now.

"I'm *so* glad you came back!" Miriam exclaimed, wrapping her slender arm about his waist.

"Fletch'll take care of the horses for you," Waddy said, turning toward the house. "We was about to set down to supper."

"If it's all the same to you," John said, "*I'll* take care of them."

"I might've knowed it," Waddy said, pride etching his voice. "You allus was that way. Took care of Rusty first, before you took care of yourself."

"I'll go in and put another piece of meat and some more potatoes on the stove," Miriam put in, proud of the fact that she was taking her ma's place in the home. "It'll be ready by the time you come in."

The barn was much the same as it had been the morning he ran away, except it wasn't in quite such good repair. The door sagged worse than before, and the roof had been patched in several places along the side facing the house. He supposed it was just as bad on the other side.

He was fumbling in the dark, trying to find the pitchfork so he could fill the manger with hay, when Fletcher came out with a lantern. The feeble yellow flame lighted a small circle around them.

"Pa thought you'd need this."

"Thanks." John took the lantern and hung it on a nail just inside the door. The faint, flickering light was enough to reveal that the pitchfork was where it had always been. If he had known that he could have found it without the help of the light. He got the fork and started to fill the manger with hay.

"How long you a-figgering to hang around here?" Fletcher demanded, bitterness in his voice.

John stopped what he was doing. He noted the hostility, but with effort, kept his own voice calm. "Can't say right now. I just got here."

"Well, the sooner you move on the better it'll be for everybody. We was a-getting along just fine, the three of us."

John put a can of oats in the feed box and patted Rusty on the nose. "I don't figger on causing nobody no trouble, Fletch," he said. "I only come to see Miriam and your pa and you. And that's the pure truth."

Fletcher moved closer and lowered his voice. "Why don't you get done a-visiting real fast like and hit the trail?"

The muscles in John's face tightened. He was in Waddy's house and Fletcher was his stepfather's son, but that didn't give him cause to throw his weight around. "Don't push me, Fletch!" he retorted icily. "You could do that back when Ma died, but you can't no more. You ain't big enough! So, just watch what you say and do. OK?"

In the dim light he could see the belligerence in his stepbrother's features. "Remember what I told ya," Fletcher rasped.

Without answering, John turned back to the big sorrel. He thought his stepbrother would go back inside now that he had spoken his mind, but Fletch waited until John had finished. Together they walked to the house.

Miriam had put another plate on the table and was standing at the stove, turning the meat in the skillet. She hadn't changed a great deal. She was about the same height as when he left and her hair was the same golden hue. Her gray eyes were soft with a tinge of sadness lurking beneath those dark lashes.

"Get washed up," she announced primly. "Supper's about ready."

He smiled. She had gotten that from Ma, though she probably didn't even realize it.

She moved her chair close to his and sat down. "I'm so glad you're back," she murmured. "You ain't going to leave no more, are you?"

"Not right away."

Fletcher's features clouded and he looked quickly down at his plate. The answer seemed to satisfy her and she began to eat.

They sat around the table for hours, asking questions about where John had been and what he had been doing. He told them how the Indians had jumped him and how Lee Corbitt had come along to chase them away. And he told them about Josiah and Belle Snyder and of her death while they were on the drive. He mentioned Gabe Gillette and the cabin he had give him in Montana Territory, but he kept quiet about the mine. He didn't want Fletcher to know about that.

Waddy remembered Gabe and told a story or two about him. "He was a fine guy," he said. "Honest as anybody you'd ever meet. A little strange some times, but he was a good man when the going got rough."

John didn't mention the bank robbery in Colorado Territory, getting shot, or the robbery he was suspected of taking part in. He knew by this time that he couldn't stay more than a couple of weeks or so; not with Fletcher here. It would only cause trouble that Waddy and Miriam didn't need. They had had enough heartache and sadness already.

John's stay at the ranch was pleasant, save for Fletch's attitude. His stepbrother didn't say anything more than he had the first night. John was sure he was afraid to for fear of Waddy's getting wind of it, but it was obvious that Fletch was eagerly awaiting the day he would leave.

Young Breckenridge fixed the sagging barn door and did some repairs around the house. He rode herd with Waddy and drove a team and wagon over to the creek a dozen miles away to cut fire-wood for winter. He had been at the Rocking Seven for almost three weeks when it happened. Fletch had been to town for supplies and came back with the team galloping.

"Pa," he cried, jerking the lathered animals to a halt. "Pa!"

Waddy hobbled out of the barn.

"What in tarnation's wrong with you?" he demanded.

"Where's John?" His voice was trembling. "We've gotta get him outta here, quick!"

By this time John and Miriam had joined the aging rancher and his son. "What's the trouble?" they asked in unison.

"There's a couple of bounty hunters in Weaverville asking questions!" he blurted. "They said they had a poster that John was wanted for robbery in Montana Territory!"

Miriam reached for John's hand and looked up into his face, her eyes pleading desperately for denial. "It ain't true, is it?" she whispered. "You didn't do what they said?"

"No, it ain't true." He squeezed her shoulders reassuringly.

"You've got to get outta here right away!" Fletch repeated. "They may even be on their way here by now!"

"John," Waddy said, his manner dark with suspicion, "I think we'd best go into the house and have us a talk!"

"I think so, too."

Hurriedly he told his stepfather the whole story, about the bank robbery Corbitt was mixed up in, getting fired from the trail herd, and Obed riding out to his place after he had been shot during the robbery attempt and dying there.

251

"I'd have gone in and faced Snyder right off," he explained, "but he ain't the sort of man you can talk to. He makes up his mind first and listens afterward."

"I know what you mean," Waddy told him. "I've seen a sight of fellers like that myself. But you don't want to be forced onto the outlaw trail. It's no good! Your pa and ma sure wouldn't want that for you."

"I don't want it, either."

"The best thing you can do is to head for Texas and Mr. Snyder's spread. By the time you get there, the chances are he'll be home and cooled off enough to hear you out. . . . Face up to him and make him understand you didn't have nothing to do with that robbery. He might give you a little trouble at first, but keep at it. He'll believe you."

John knew, even as his stepfather talked, that he would have to do what he said. It was the only way he could avoid being on the run the rest of his life, worrying every night that someone might sneak up on him while he slept.

"I'll get my gear together."

Miriam cried as he was leaving. It was all he could do to tear himself away from her and saddle Rusty.

"You'll be back, won't you?" she managed.

"I'll be back!" With that he rode off.

22

It had been late afternoon when Fletcher Ross dashed recklessly back to the Rocking Seven with the disturbing news that bounty hunters were on John's trail. Young Breckenridge wasted at least an hour talking with his stepfather and Miriam and getting his gear together. He hadn't been on his way long before darkness settled in upon the prairie. With the setting of the sun, a chill swept in from the north, and the youthful rider shivered. But he could not stop now—not until he put more miles between himself and his pursuers.

The moon came out presently, washing the silent land with a soft, gentle light. It was not bright enough to cause shadows, but made him plainly visible should anyone be on his trail. If there had been a place to hide, he would have stopped, but he dared not risk it. He had to keep moving.

Toward midnight clouds drifted in and he felt more secure. Not long after he came to a dry creek with a few scattered trees along each bank. There wasn't enough cover near the trail, but there was promise of it in other directions. He headed west until he came to a stretch of rough ground to provide himself and his horse a measure of safety. There he spent the night, his bedroll stretched out in a narrow ravine that couldn't be seen from the trail. After midnight the wind came up and it grew colder, laying a skim of ice on the puddles in the low places nearby. Shivering, John wakened and got his heavy sheepskin coat, pulling it over him.

The following morning he was up at dawn, fried bacon and flapjacks over a small fire, and boiled coffee for breakfast. For two days he headed south. It was his plan to miss Ogallala in order to save time, but he changed his mind and turned west toward the rip-roaring Nebraska town where the Norvalls and Gabe Gillette lived.

It would be good to see the family that had nursed him back to health. And he really owed Gabe half the dust he had taken from the mine. The old man had insisted that he had everything he needed, but he hadn't looked like it. His clothes and the haggard set to his features indicated he was hard put to buy the necessities of life.

Another day's ride and John reached Ogallala. He went into town toward evening and stopped in front of the hotel. Matt Norvall was behind the desk when John opened the door and entered the long lobby. His hat was perched on the back of his head and a smile lighted his lean, bronzed face.

"John!" his friend cried, rushing out from behind the counter and hurrying across the well-scrubbed pine floor to meet him. "It's good to see you!"

Breckenridge took Norvall's work-worn hand in his own fist. "How're you doing, Matt?"

"Tolerable." He turned his head to call for his wife and daughter. "Rebecca! Helen! Come here! We've got company!" He turned back to John. "They're really going to be surprised!"

In a moment the door at the far end of the lobby opened and they came out, Helen a step or two behind her mother. Rebecca stopped inside the door, staring at their guest. She had been wiping her reddened hands on the corner of her apron, but that movement, too, was frozen.

"John!" she exclaimed, her voice shrill. "I never would've guessed it was you!"

He wanted to throw his arms about her the way he would have greeted his own ma if she were alive. But that would have been too bold. Instead, he took her hand warmly. "It's right good to see you, Ma'am."

Helen hung back with a shyness she had never shown around him before. She allowed herself a quick look in his direction before lowering her gaze. She had changed more than her parents in the year he had been away. Her figure was beginning to round and soften beneath the sheathlike cotton dress. She was carrying herself with the quiet dignity of a young woman, looking and acting more like her ma and older sister. But, as far as he was concerned, she was going to be more beautiful than either of them.

The little girl was still very much present in Helen; her dancing eyes were more used to laughter and the joy of life than the trials of adults. But the young woman was there as well, demanding recognition and acceptance. John knew that in a couple of years half the young men in the area would be traipsing to the hotel in the hope that she would favor them with a smile. But now, she came forward hesitantly, holding out her hand.

"And here's my nurse!" John said warmly.

Her face seemed to come alive. "Elizabeth ain't here," she volunteered. "She ran off with Charlie Sims and got married."

"You and your pa and ma are the ones I came to see."

Her cheeks flushed crimson.

"I wanted to see you and I wanted to find out how *Robinson Crusoe* turned out."

Her voice was so soft he strained to hear the words. "I . . . I stopped reading it when . . . when you left."

Her pa didn't seem to notice the exchange. "I'll bet you're starved, John. Come on in the kitchen and have supper with us. Rebecca will put on another plate."

"Supper isn't quite ready," she said, "but you must eat with us."

"I'll stable Rusty in the livery barn and take care of an errand I have in town." He glanced at Rebecca. "Would thirty minutes be too late?"

He left the horse at the stable and went over to the saloon where he had been shot. The bartender recognized him immediately and came over as soon as he was free.

"I wondered if you wouldn't be along," he said.

"Does the old mountain man, Gabe Gillette, still come in here?" Breckenridge asked.

"That's right, he was a friend of your pa's. He died last winter. Took sick during a storm. He was holed up in that little cabin of his on the edge of town. When the snow let up so's somebody could look in on him, he was gone."

"I'm right sorry to hear that."

"Everybody was." He eyed John quizzically. "He weren't no kin of yourn, was he?"

John shook his head. "Like you said, he used to know my pa."

One of the customers called for a beer and

the bartender drew it before turning back to John. "That boss of yourn was here three or four days ago," he said. "That's how I knowed you'd be a-coming."

Breckenridge tried not to show his surprise. "What was he doing?"

"Drinking hard. What else? . . . He and that feller who was with him said they stopped in town to get the horses on their chuck wagon shod and stopped here for a couple of drinks. Like usual, they didn't get no farther. About closing time I told them I couldn't serve them no more and they'd have to leave. . . . They started tearing up the place and wouldn't quit till the marshal got here and threw them in jail. The next morning he went to tell them they could go if they'd pay the damages, but they wasn't there. They'd busted out, got their team outta the livery stable, and took off. We ain't seen hide nor hair of them since."

"I didn't reckon he'd have no wagon, now," John muttered. "Getting robbed and all. I figgered he'd have sold it, like last year."

"Well, they had a wagon," the bartender repeated. "And they said they stopped here to get the blacksmith to take care of their team."

John thanked him and went out. If the story were true, and there was no reason the bartender would lie, Snyder would be stopping at one of the other towns south of Ogallala. The rancher had changed since Belle died, with his drinking and all, but he still took care of his horses. No one could deny that. It would be like him to get the team shod as soon as they needed it.

Breckenridge had a long talk with the Norvall family that night, sitting with them around the table in their kitchen. They were sorry to learn that he had to leave in the morning.

"You could stay a few more days, couldn't you?" Helen asked.

"I'd like to, but I've got to catch up with Snyder. The longer I stay here, the harder that'll be."

For her, disappointment blurred the joy of his being with them. The rest of the evening she had little to say.

They got up early at the hotel, and Rebecca served John breakfast before he left. He was sitting down at the table when Helen came in wearing one of her best dresses. Her hair was neatly combed.

"I wanted to say good-bye."

Leaving the Norvalls was almost as difficult as leaving Waddy and Miriam, but it had to be done if he was to catch up with Snyder and Todd, or whoever was with the rancher. He left as quickly as he could to keep from showing his own emotion, picked up his horse, and set out for Kelly, the nearest community south of Ogallala. It was a hard day's ride away, but compared to the distance between other towns it was fairly close.

He cantered into the sleepy little village an hour before sunset, just as the general store was closing. The clerk and an older man John assumed was the proprietor carried sacks of flour or sugar out to the spring wagon and waved good-bye to the rancher who was on the seat with the lines in his hand. Then they started moving a row of barrels that lined the porch, rolling them into the building so they could lock up. John was looking for the livery barn when he saw a familiar figure on the boardwalk across the street hunkered into a grimy sheepskin with his hat pulled low over his eyes. He was making for the nearest saloon: Josiah Snyder!

John stopped Rusty at the nearest hitchng post, tied the reins quickly, and strode down the street after his former boss.

"Josiah!" he called out.

The rancher turned at the sound of his voice.

"You!" he snarled. "I thought I was done with you!"

"And I thought I was done with you," John retorted icily. "But it turns out we ain't." For an instant their eyes met and fought in silence.

"Breckenridge!" Snyder said, "I been on the road for a long time. I'm tired and I've got a powerful thirst. Just git yourself wherever you was a-heading and leave me alone! You've caused me more trouble now than any one man ought to have to take!"

"I've got some questions to get answered first and some things straightened around!" The words came out cold and hard as stone. "I didn't have nothing to do with stealing your money. You ought to know that. Why'd you put out a reward for me?"

Snyder moved closer, his hand resting ominously on the butt of his gun. John saw it and stepped backward so there would be a little space between them if it came to a shoot-out. He didn't know why, but he felt that his former boss was weighing his chances of getting off the first shot.

"I wouldn't try if I was you," John cautioned.

"You don't scare me!" the rancher snapped. In spite of the bravado in his voice he lowered his gun hand. "I don't know what you're talking about when you say I put up a reward for ya. I didn't do

259

nothing like that! I should've, but I wouldn't on account of Belle! She put a heap of store by you, even iffen you didn't deserve it."

"Somebody put up a reward for my arrest and you're the only one I know who'd have done it."

Snyder's face was livid. "You calling me a liar?"

"Put any name on it you want to. You went to the marshal in Red Cedar, Montana Territory, and made him believe I was in on stealing your herd money, but I wasn't. I was thirty miles away when it happened."

"Then you ain't got nothing to worry about."

"That ain't true. A couple of bounty hunters was after me, and they don't come around for nothing. You know that!"

The muscles about Snyder's mouth tightened. Then he seemed to relax. "There's been some mistake," he said, smiling coldly. "I'll go over to see the marshal here and get it straightened out."

"*We'll* go over to the marshal and get it straightened out," John corrected him. "And we won't wait till you get drunk and forget about it. We're going right now." He took his former boss by the arm and started down the street in the direction of the jail.

"I gotta meet a friend."

"He'll be there when we get back." They crossed the street and continued up the walk. "Josiah, I'm a-telling you straight," he continued, more conciliatory than before. "I didn't have nothing to do with that robbery. I was up in the hills at the cabin old Gabe Gillette gave me. I never knew nothing about the trouble down in Red Cedar

260

till Obed come a-riding in with a bullet in his back." John stopped and faced him.

The rancher was almost apologetic. "I don't know who caused the trouble for ya, but I didn't have nothing to do with it."

They reached the jail and tried the door, but it was locked.

"He ain't here now," Snyder said. "We'll have to see him tomorrow."

John paused. "You won't leave town before we do?"

"I can't. I've got to get my team shod."

Breckenridge started back to the place where Rusty was tied, but stopped and faced Snyder. "You pull out on me and I'll be on your tail till I catch you. Just remember that!"

The rancher swore. "You're a-making it awful hard for us to get along."

"I want you to know how things are!"

The rancher stormed back in the direction of the saloon, his sharp Mexican spurs clattering noisily on the boardwalk.

John made his way to his horse, mounted, and rode out of town. He had intended to spend the night at a local hotel but after the encounter with his former boss, he changed his mind. It would be too easy for the rancher to alert the marshal to the fact that he was in Kelly. He could be taken in bed and thrown into jail where it would be his word against Snyder's. It would be better to find a quiet place several miles from town and make camp. It wouldn't be so comfortable, but it would be safer.

He found a narrow tree-covered gully three miles from town and made camp in a spot that was out of the wind. Sleep was slow in coming, and he lay there, trying to sort things out. Why would Snyder be driving a wagon back to Texas? Last year he had sold the chuck wagon after the storm wiped out his herd. The rancher hated driving a team. He cursed the times when he couldn't travel by horseback, but had to use a team and wagon. Why would he choose to take the wagon all the way to Texas when he could have sold it in Montana Territory and ridden his horse south to the Walking S? There had to be a reason; there usually was a reason for everything. But in this case he didn't know what it could be.

He awakened in the predawn chill, built a fire, and fixed breakfast. When he got in to town, the dirty little collection of buildings was still asleep. Here and there a lamp winked in a window and smoke drifted skyward from the kitchen stove, but most places were dark and silent. His pulse quickened as the big sorrel trotted up the main street. He was certain of one thing: He was in town early enough to intercept Snyder unless the rancher had taken off the night before, which wasn't likely. Now, maybe he could get things straightened out.

He stopped Rusty in front of the livery stable and dismounted. The hostler was somewhere in the big structure, but he was asleep and John had to walk the length of the barn to locate him.

"Just a minute," the hand muttered sleepily. "I'll get the lantern."

"I ain't going to leave my horse," John said. "I'm looking for the wagon them fellers from Texas drove in."

The hostler swore. "Waking a body up to find a wagon," he growled. "It's out back. But don't you take nothing from it. We got us a marshal here!"

262

"I ain't figgering on taking nothing."

John opened the big door and looked out. The sun hadn't come up yet but the darkness of night was fast disappearing and he could see the varnish on a new wagon sitting in the lot behind the frame building. There was a name in small letters on the tail gate: Strausacker's Wagon Works, Red Cedar, Montana Territory.

"I don't see it," he said. "The one I'm a-looking for is an older wagon, made in Texas."

"You got eyes, ain't ya?"

"I tell you, I know Snyder's chuck wagon," John retorted. "And that ain't it!"

At the sound of their voices there was a stirring inside. "Who's out there?" someone in the chuck wagon demanded roughly.

"You ought to know, Snyder!" John retorted. "We have us a meeting this morning. Remember?"

A moment later Snyder crawled out, loosening the gun in his holster. He still stank of stale whiskey, and his face was flushed from the drinking of the night before. But at least he appeared to be sober.

"I know why you're here," he blurted. "It weren't enough to rob me once. You had to sneak out here and see if I had anything left you could steal!"

"If I'd been bent on robbing you," John told him, trying to hold his temper, "I wouldn't have woke up the hostler to find out where your wagon was."

The rancher seemed only partially satisfied. "What do you want with my wagon?"

"I was supposed to see you this morning and I wanted to be sure you didn't run out on me."

"The marshal ain't even out of bed yet," Snyder replied darkly.

"I can wait." John walked to the rear of the wagon and traced the well-formed letters with a finger. "How come you got a new wagon?" he asked suddenly.

"None of your business!"

"You bought a new one last spring, and it was in good shape. At least it was when you fired me on the way up."

Snyder shifted nervously from one foot to the other. "Had trouble with it in Montana Territory," he said lamely. "Figgered I'd best get a new one."

"Last year ya *sold* the chuck wagon after ya lost the herd in that storm. This time you was robbed and lost all the money you got out of them cattle. Chances are ya won't get nobody to back ya again, come spring. *How come you needed a new wagon?*"

"Like I said, it ain't none of your business!" Sweat pearled on his puffy face.

"Strausacker," John said aloud. "Ain't that the outfit that makes them special wagons? The ones with the false floors?"

The rancher swallowed hard. "I don't know what you're a-talking about."

"I think ya do. Let's have us a look!"

Snyder spraddled his legs and his hand moved ominously closer to the handle of his Colt .45. "You keep away from this wagon!"

"If you don't let me look, we'll have the marshal see what he can find!"

Snyder bellowed with rage and jerked his weapon from his holster. His Colt was coming up when John drew and fired. The slug caught

Snyder's gun arm before he could squeeze the trigger. He dropped the heavy six-gun and grabbed the wound with his other hand. Breckenridge stepped forward and picked up the weapon, a sudden nausea sweeping over him. He had been afraid this would happen, but he hadn't wanted it to come to this. He had done everything he could to avoid a gunfight with his former boss.

"*I'll kill you for this!*" the wounded man said between clenched teeth.

"I didn't want to do it, Josiah!" John protested. "But you drew first."

Neither had noticed the hostler until he spoke. "That's right. I seen it!"

"Let's get you to a doctor!" John put in, all thought of proving his own innocence gone for the moment.

"Keep your hands off me!"

Before Breckenridge could reach the rancher, Snyder turned quickly away and stepped to the other side of the wagon. His former trail boss started to follow, but before he had moved two steps another shot rang out, followed by the thud of a heavy body falling. John and the hostler dashed around the corner of the wagon and saw Snyder motionless on the ground, a derringer in his hand and a widening pool of blood staining the bare soil near his head.

"He's shot himself!" John cried. "Get the doctor and the marshal!"

The young hostler scurried off.

The sound of the shooting brought several men running to the back of the livery stable. Snyder was dead when they got there.

"I know you," the marshal said when he approached John. "You're the trail boss who robbed him up in Montana Territory. He was talking to me about you last night. I was on my way over here to go with him and arrest you when Sam came and told me he done committed suicide. And that's one I can't figger out!"

"I'm the feller he *claimed* robbed him," John said. "But I didn't have nothing to do with it, no more than I had something to do with shooting him in the head. That's why I've been follering him—so's we could get this mess straightened out."

"That's for the judge. Come along."

John stood his ground. "Have a look in that wagon first. It's one of them new ones they make up in Montana with a false floor in the front so gold can be stashed away.

"The way I figger it," he continued, "Snyder hired some known outlaws as drovers so he could stage the robbery after he was paid. Then he doublecrossed the thieves and killed them so's they wouldn't get their share of the gold. . . . He robbed his own self, just like he killed his self."

The marshal laughed scornfully. "Now, why would a man go to all that trouble when it was his anyway?"

"That's just it," Breckenridge persisted. "The money wasn't his. Not all of it, anyway. Most of them longhorns in his herd belonged to his neighbors. He was a-taking them north for half the profit. . . . I reckon he just got greedy."

"We'll soon see." The marshal borrowed a hammer from Sam at the livery barn and loosed the front half of the wagon floor. It was obvious by the way he worked that he didn't believe he would find anything. He kept one eye on John to be sure he didn't leave. When he finally removed one of the boards, however, he gasped in surprise. There were heavy canvas sacks between the two floors filled with gold coins. "What do ya know?" he exclaimed. "You was right!"

"That had to be the answer. It was the only one that made any sense."

The marshal took the gold over to the bank and left it for safe keeping till he could make arrangements to get it to its rightful owners. Then he went to the hotel, taking John along to point out Snyder's companion. Bruce Todd was in the dining room having breakfast when they approached. He shoved his chair back from the table.

"You!" he exploded. "I didn't think you'd have nerve to come around after what you did!"

"I didn't do nothing. That's why I'm here. We come to tell you that your boss is dead."

Todd's stare was icy. "What happened?" he demanded of John. "Was it you who killed him?"

"He killed his own self," the marshal said. "We wondered if you could tell us why?"

Todd pulled in a deep breath. "I don't know much."

"Let's go to my office where we can talk," the marshal said. They left the dining room and went up the street to the jail.

"Now," the officer began as they sat around his desk, "what can you tell us?"

"After the robbery," Todd said, "the marshal up Montana way wanted to arrest Elim Haynes for being in on it, but Mr. Snyder wouldn't hear to that. Said Elim didn't have nothing to do with it. It plumb surprised me the way he stuck up for him."

"Then what happened?"

"After we got the new wagon, Elim started

south with us. I figgered him and Snyder was friends, but they was a-stalking each other like a pair of mountain lions. We hadn't gone fifty miles till there was a showdown and Mr. Snyder killed him."

John nodded. "It all adds up. Don't it?"

The marshal rolled a cigarette. "Appears like you was right. Snyder had to get rid of Elim Haynes to keep his secret."

"What're you two a-talking about?" Todd wanted to know.

The officer told him about the false bottom in the wagon with its cargo of gold coins.

"I don't get it! Snyder was the only one who got near that wagon. That means the gold was never stole."

"That's the way I figger," John put in.

"I thought Snyder was all-fired calm about losing everything two years in a row." Todd said, "He didn't even go out and tie one on like I thought he would." He paused. "But I don't see how it was pulled off. He didn't have nothing to do with stealing the money. According to what he told the marshal, he surprised young Haynes, and Obed and Corbitt robbing him and he killed all three of them, but somebody else got off with the money. He said he figgered it was you, John. There's even a wanted poster out for you."

"The money in that wagon proves Snyder was in on it," the marshal said. He turned to John. "I'm more sure than ever that Haynes and his brother and Snyder had this deal cooked up back in Texas. Elim and Little Ike brought them other two, Corbitt and Obed, in on it. Snyder and the Haynes brothers planned to kill Corbitt and Obed after the holdup, to blame the robbery on them.

But Snyder doublecrossed them and killed Little Ike, too. He probably figgered on killing Elim, but he didn't get him like he planned. That was why he was killed after they started south."

They buried Snyder that afternoon. Breckenridge, the undertaker, and Todd were the only ones there. They would have lowered the casket and filled in the grave without any service, but John didn't want that. He said a prayer before they scooped in the dirt. He knew it wouldn't do any good, but he didn't do it for Snyder. He said the prayer because he knew Belle would have wanted it—and it helped him to feel a little better.

He waited at the cemetery till the grave was filled in and the board with Snyder's name and dates was in place. Then he mounted Rusty and rode off. He was sorry it had come to this, but he had felt it would, sooner or later. In spite of the heaviness of his own heart because of his former boss, he felt clean inside. He had been vindicated. No longer would he have to fear every stranger who approached who might turn out to be a bounty hunter.

John didn't know where he was going next. It didn't matter. He was free to go where he pleased.

Other Living Books Bestsellers

THE MAN WHO COULD DO NO WRONG by Charles E. Blair with John and Elizabeth Sherrill. He built one of the largest churches in America . . . then he made a mistake. This is the incredible story of Pastor Charles E. Blair, accused of massive fraud. A book "for error-prone people in search of the Christian's secret for handling mistakes." 07–4002 $3.50.

GIVERS, TAKERS AND OTHER KINDS OF LOVERS by Josh McDowell. This book bypasses vague generalities about love and sex and gets right down to basic questions: Whatever happened to sexual freedom? What's true love like? What is your most important sex organ? Do men respond differently than women? If you're looking for straight answers about God's plan for love and sexuality then this book was written for you. 07–1031 $2.50.

MORE THAN A CARPENTER by Josh McDowell. This best selling author thought Christians must be "out of their minds." He put them down. He argued against their faith. But eventually he saw that his arguments wouldn't stand up. In this book, Josh focuses upon the person who changed his life — Jesus Christ. 07–4552 $2.50.

HIND'S FEET ON HIGH PLACES by Hannah Hurnard. A classic allegory which has sold more than a million copies! 07–1429 $3.50.

THE CATCH ME KILLER by Bob Erler with John Souter. Golden gloves, black belt, green beret, silver badge. Supercop Bob Erler had earned the colors of manhood. Now can he survive prison life? An incredible true story of forgiveness and hope. 07–0214 $3.50.

WHAT WIVES WISH THEIR HUSBANDS KNEW ABOUT WOMEN by Dr. James Dobson. By the best selling author of *DARE TO DISCIPLINE* and *THE STRONG-WILLED CHILD*, here's a vital book that speaks to the unique emotional needs and aspirations of today's woman. An immensely practical, interesting guide. 07–7896 $2.95.

PONTIUS PILATE by Dr. Paul Maier. This fascinating novel is about one of the most famous Romans in history — the man who declared Jesus innocent but who nevertheless sent him to the cross. This powerful biblical novel gives you a unique insight into the life and death of Jesus. 07–4852 $3.95.

BROTHER OF THE BRIDE by Donita Dyer. This exciting sequel to *THE BRIDE'S ESCAPE* tells of the faith of a proud, intelligent Armenian family whose Christian heritage stretched back for centuries. A story of suffering, separation, valor, victory, and reunion. 07–0179 $2.95.

LIFE IS TREMENDOUS by Charlie Jones. Believing that enthusiasm makes the difference, Jones shows how anyone can be happy, involved, relevant, productive, healthy, and secure in the midst of a high-pressure, commercialized, automated society. 07–2184 $2.50.

HOW TO BE HAPPY THOUGH MARRIED by Dr. Tim LaHaye. One of America's most successful marriage counselors gives practical, proven advice for marital happiness. 07–1499 $2.95.

The books listed are available at your bookstore. If unavailable, send check with order to cover retail price plus 10% for postage and handling to:

Tyndale House Publishers, Inc.
Box 80
Wheaton, Illinois 60189

Prices and availability subject to change without notice. Allow 4–6 weeks for delivery.